THE … T *NUTS*:

"A SI … DRAMA . . . bares its teeth right from the start and plunges forward . . . packs a punch!"

—*New York Daily News*

"FASCINATING . . . the most gripping courtroom drama since Agatha Christie's *Witness for the Prosecution* and Herman Wouk's *The Caine Mutiny Court Martial.*"

—Clive Barnes, *New York Post*

"A SUPERLATIVELY TENSE COURTROOM DRAMA!" —*International Herald Tribune*

"A SALVO OF EMOTIONAL TRACER BULLETS . . . A cross between *One Flew Over the Cuckoo's Nest* and *Whose Life Is It, Anyway?*"

—*Newsweek*

"THE TENSION BUILDS AND HOLDS . . . *NUTS* IS WONDERFULLY SANE."

—*San Francisco Chronicle*

NUTS

A Novel by
Claudia Reilly

Screenplay by
Tom Topor and Darryl Ponicsan
& Alvin Sargent

Based upon the Play by Tom Topor

published by
the Paperback Division of
W.H. Allen & Co. Plc

A Star Book
Published in 1988
by the Paperback Division of
W.H. Allen & Co. Plc
44 Hill Street, London W1X 8LB

Published by arrangement with
NAL PENGUIN INC., New York

Printed and bound in Great Britain by
Anchor Brendon Ltd, Tiptree, Essex

ISBN 0 352 32267 5

PUBLISHER'S NOTE

This book is a work of fiction. Names, characters, places, and incidents either are the product of the author's imagination or are used fictitiously, and any resemblance to actual persons, living or dead, events, or locales is entirely coincidental.

ONE

It was only nine in the morning, and he hadn't even started work yet, but already Aaron Levinsky knew he was in for a bad day. Not that Levinsky ever had good days, exactly. When you were forty years old and trying to support a wife and three kids on what a Legal Aid attorney makes, you didn't have good days. Maybe you had bearable days when your wife forgot to remind you that your stupid, bleeding-heart liberalism was dragging her into poverty; maybe you even had almost good days when one of the murderers you were defending didn't try to insist he was innocent on the grounds that he could have sworn his victim's heart was still beating after he'd slugged the guy over the head with a baseball bat twenty times; but honest-to-God good days? Hah! Still, even Levinsky—a self-proclaimed schlemiel—knew a particularly bad day when he saw one coming and this one was heading his way like a drunk teenager on a stolen motorcyle.

To start with, on the subway ride into Manhattan this morning, Levinsky had managed to catch a glimpse of his own reflection in the train's window. What he saw had made him gasp, for the face looking back at him was that of a middle-aged failure: bleary-eyed, exhausted, wrinkled, and drained. Well, the face was explained by the late hours Levinsky kept trying to help his clients get back out on the streets so they could commit more crimes. But what was to explain the caved-in shoulders, the gray beard gone frazzled with indifference, the worn-out clothes, the paunch beginning to crawl over the belt? Clearly, Levinsky had given up on life. But how and when and why? He really didn't know.

Levinsky had gotten off the train at Lexington Avenue and considered walking up the steep flight of stairs, yet somewhow he hadn't found the willpower for the climb. So he had ridden up on the safe, familiar steps of the escalator, watching as men ten or fifteen years his senior scampered up the stairs. These men, Levinsky knew, were successes. On their way to do work they believed in, off to seize the day with gusto. Levinsky had to turn away from them, for he was on his way to a rundown, decrepit arraignment court in the heart of Manhattan's highest crime district. There he would have to push, shove, and shout his way through endless sessions of plea bargaining involving the endless stream of court-appointed clients. And for what? Just to earn the privilege of taking the subway home at the end of the day so his wife could greet him with the words, "You're late. Go fix yourself a peanut butter sandwich or something. I already threw your dinner away."

Leaving the subway station behind him, Levinsky had walked downtown in a state that was either signaling a midlife crisis or a minor nervous breakdown. It was a sunny September morning, but the sun didn't seem to apply to Levinsky. He watched it cast its light on the pretty young women who passed him by without a glance; he saw it shine on the junior executives who were quickly working their way to the top. But for Levinsky himself, there was only darkness.

Then the worst thing possible had happened. As Levinsky stood at a street corner waiting for a light to turn, a shining black limousine had pulled up alongside him and a smoked-colored window in the backseat came down. Suddenly, the smiling face of an old buddy from law school, Seymour Cohen, had appeared at the window. "Hey Levinsky!" Cohen had shouted. "You still trying to save the world?"

Levinsky had laughed and tried to think of some witty remark to toss back at Cohen, but when he'd opened his mouth, no words came out, and in a moment Cohen's limousine was cruising back down the street. Levinsky had remained on the curb, stunned and shaken, watching the limousine until it was only a gleaming black dot in the distance.

Trembling, Levinsky had finally moved on. So Cohen—at one time almost as much of a schlemiel as Levinsky himself—had become a hotshot in the legal world while Levinsky had become a joke. Levinsky wanted to scream out in protest. Hadn't Cohen been the very person who had talked him into going to work for Legal Aid back in the days when he had been considering corporate law? How had it happened that in the seventeen years since Cohen and Levinsky had roomed together at Columbia, Cohen had come to develop common sense while Levinsky had only developed ulcers? And just how many ulcers was it going to take before Levinsky admitted that not only was the world past salvation, but so was he?

The final ill omen Levinsky had about his day had come just as he'd arrived at work. His body had been sweating, his head pounding as he'd pushed open the graffiti-covered doors of the ancient courthouse and made his way along a crowded, narrow hallway to a coffee machine. He'd plunked fifty cents into the thing. *Nada.* Desperately in need of caffeine, he'd tossed in two more quarters. This time the machine had spewed forth a stream of putrid brown liquid but failed to produce a paper cup. Levinsky had felt an impulse to kick out at the machine, but figured the way his day was going he'd probably break his toe, so instead he had merely let a whimper of pain leak from his throat.

Now, about to enter the courtroom, Levinsky wondered what else was going to go wrong today. Maybe he'd get fired? One of his clients would shoot him? Surely, some terrible fate awaited him. His shoulders slumped low. Whatever was going to happen to him, he was certain he wanted no part of it.

But then, very few lawyers would have wanted to face what awaited Aaron Levinsky that day. For Levinsky was about to be handed the hardest, scariest, and most mystifying case of his career. And while the case wasn't going to give him the chance to save the world, it certainly was going to force him to do his damnedest to save not only himself, but also the most intriguing woman he would ever meet in his life: Claudia Faith Draper.

The holding tank cell in the basement of the courthouse was jammed full of women prisoners waiting to be brought before the judge. There were black women, white women, brown women, and yellow women. Due to both the crowded conditions in the cell and the length of time they had been forced to spend together, the women had developed a kind of camaraderie. They formed groups together—groups that had more to do with their crimes than their races. The first-time offenders huddled together at the rusty, iron bars of the cell and stood white-knuckled with fear as they looked for the guard who was supposed to come for them; while those who had been to court before either sat on benches chatting quietly about favorite characters on TV soap operas or sprawled across the concrete floor and bragged to each other about new and improved ways to steal leather coats from Bloomingdale's.

Only one of the women sat off by herself. Claudia Draper, a thirty-five-year-old woman dressed in men's pajamas and a too-large bathrobe, was curled up in a corner of the cell with her head between her knees. Her brown hair was snarled and matted; a filthy bandage was wrapped around her right hand; and her body was so thin that her bones seemed to be trying to push their way out of her flesh. The other women in the cell—many of whom were about to face charges for violent crimes—were afraid of Claudia and kept their distance. They presumed, correctly, that she had been brought over to the courthouse from a psychiatric ward, and if she was content to sit like a zombie in silence, they were content to let her do it.

At last two guards appeared at the cell door. While one of them stood watch in the corridor with his hand on his holster, the other entered with a clipboard to which was attached a list of names of the first women to be taken to the courtroom.

The guard had to shout over the women's conversations: "Gutterez, Luna."

A young Spanish woman shoved her way to the front of the tank.

"Washington, Tyra."

After spitting out a wad of gum onto the floor, a black woman came over to the guard.

"Kirk, Claudia."

There was no response for a time. The guard glanced around and was just about to repeat the name when suddenly Claudia raised her bandaged hand over her head and looked up for the first time that morning. The guard and all of the women in the cell were surprised to see that beneath the mop of hair was a beautiful face with piercing blue eyes and wide, high cheekbones.

Claudia stood up and joined the others as the guard called out three more names. Then all six women were led by the guard into the hallway where they were instructed to form a single-file line between the guard with the clipboard and his partner.

The women walked along the corridor like reluctant soldiers about to face a battle they knew they couldn't possibly win. First they passed other holding tanks containing women, some of whom waved or sent thumbs-up signals, and then they passed the men's tanks, where the greetings were of a different variety.

The men were pressed against their cell bars with their arms reaching out to the women. Some merely hooted and whistled, but others rubbed their groins and moaned with desire. Most of the women ignored the men's pleadings, but Claudia Draper turned and looked toward the tanks with unblinking eyes.

They think they can hide behind their two-thousand dollar suits from Brooks Brothers or their wives from Scarsdale. I walk by them in the lobby of the Walnut Room, my gold sequined dress cut so low on my breasts that I have to breathe slowly to keep my nipples in place. They are rich, powerful men who give discreet winks instead of catcalls, who think they are good, God-fearing Re-

publicans, fathers, and husbands, but I know better. I know when their wives go off to the ladies' room, these men will come to me with hundred-dollar bills tucked ever so carefully between their business cards. Oh, they think they believe in truth, justice, and the American way, but I know all they believe in are my breasts. . . .

One of the guards touched Claudia on her shoulder to pull her out of her trance. She jumped the moment his fingers reached the material of her robe, spun toward him, and gave him a look of such rage and pain that for a moment he thought of calling out to his partner, but then she blinked and her anger disappeared as quickly and absolutely as it had come. Her eyes went dull, her head sank low, and without a word she moved on in line with the other women.

Past the men's tanks was a winding metal staircase. The woman clattered up the steps until they came to a door marked PRISONERS' ENTRANCE. There the guards who had brought them up from the holding tank transferred them over to another guard who led the women into the courtroom.

The courtroom was large, hot, decidedly squalid, and packed full of prisoners, spectators, and lawyers—many of whom were moving about or shouting out to each other, so that a feeling of both urgency and chaos seemed to fill the room. A court officer stood near the spectators and pleaded with them to be quiet, but these mothers, wives, girlfriends, husbands, fathers, friends, employers, and victims of the prisoners all were intent on getting a message to the prisoners and either ignored or didn't hear the officer's words.

Aaron Levinsky was leafing madly through a huge pile of case folders as Claudia and the other women entered the room. The next case coming up on the docket was his, but as yet he couldn't locate the prisoner's folder. He put on a pair of horn-rimmed glasses in an effort to read his own handwriting and looked up in exasperation when he realized that the lenses on his glasses were too smeared to see through.

Taking the glasses off to clean them, Levinsky caught sight of Claudia as the courtroom guard led her and the other women to a long bench already full of prisoners waiting for their cases to be called. He noticed her wild hair, dirty bandage, and baggy pajamas. He started to smirk, but then she turned her staring eyes his way and something about the emptiness and loss in them made him drop the smirk and look away in embarrassment. No doubt about it, they were not so different from the eyes he had seen reflected back at him in the train window glass earlier that morning.

Still, empathy or no empathy, Levinsky sent up a silent thank-you to a God he no longer believed in for the fact that Claudia wasn't one of his clients. He'd had to deal with his share of psychos over the years and considered them the bane of his legal existence. There was nothing quite like defending a person who insisted on being referred to as "Lucifer, King of Damnation, Protector of the Dark Universe."

So where was that folder? All Levinsky needed was to walk up before the bench unprepared and by tomorrow he'd be out selling pencils on the street alongside King Lucifer and the nut in men's pajamas. For, no matter how wild the spectators in the back of the court might be, Judge Lawrence Box expected and received absolute respect in the front of the court. To go before the judge and ask for a delay in order to hunt for a client's folder was unthinkable.

Judge Lawrence Box was one of those people who, although only a few years older than Levinsky, had an aura of grave responsibility. The judge was fast, efficient, and absolutely determined to get through as many cases a day as humanly—or inhumanly—possible. And while a lot of people (including Levinsky) saw arraignment courts as second rate because they lacked the decorum of trial courts, Judge Box believed in his court's importance and brought a kind of militaristic sense of absolute process to his work. Surrounded by a clerk and a bridgeman who anticipated his needs, the judge never let things slow down. Levinsky held the judge responsible for his ulcers and gray hair, but he had a grudging respect for the man and really dreaded the thought of approaching the bench unprepared.

As Levinsky searched once more for the folder, the judge finished up a case. "Five hundred dollars or thirty days," he told a defendant. "Three weeks to pay."

The courtroom clerk, seated to the left of the judge, checked a calendar. "October fourteen."

The judge nodded. "By that date."

And that was that. The judge closed the defendant's folder, the bridgeman hurriedly picked it up, and it was laid across the clerk's desk for stamping and processing. Another faster-than-a-speeding-bullet case had come and gone and now it was Levinsky's turn.

"Calendar twenty-one," the clerk called out immediately. "People *versus* Roosevelt Davis, docket number 8483, September nineteen. Defendant is charged with grand larceny. Does the defendant waive the reading of the rights and charges?"

"Yes he does," Levinsky shouted out, knowing how Judge Box felt about long, drawn-out recitations in his courtroom.

Roosevelt Davis, a large, burly young black man, was led toward the defendant's table. He stared at Levinsky contemptuously, clearly not pleased that his rights weren't to be read to him. Levinsky didn't notice the stare, though, as he was still rifling through his stack of folders.

"For the people, Saul Kreiglitz," the clerk said quickly. "For the defendant, Aaron Levinsky."

Suddenly, miraculously, Levinsky found Davis's folder. His face almost broke into a smile as he rushed—his stack of folders filling his arms—to join Saul Kreiglitz in the front.

Kreiglitz, one of the few lawyers in Manhattan to make almost as little money as Levinsky, was waiting at the side of the bench with his own set of folders. He grinned at Levinsky's messy stack. The two men had known each other for ten harried years. They were as friendly as two overworked, dead-tired lawyers could be who worked the opposite ends of the pole. Each knew where the other stood on every judicial issue, which made their plea-bargaining sessions not only fast, but telegraphic at times.

Levinsky was the first to begin the bargaining this morning. He stood close to Kreiglitz and whispered so that neither the judge nor the defendant could hear: "So, what do you gimme on him?"

Kreiglitz shrugged. "I'll give him a misdemeanor."

Levinsky tried his best shot: "He was an accessory. How 'bout disorderly conduct?"

But Kreiglitz only grimaced, as Levinsky had presumed he would. Pointing to his own folder on Roosevelt Davis, Kreiglitz said, "C'mon, Aaron. He shows a prior."

Levinsky nodded. Maybe with another lawyer he would have kept going, tried to point out extenuating circumstances, but with Kreiglitz this was pointless. When you have played poker with someone enough times over the years, you know when they're bluffing and when they're not. Plea bargaining was a kind of poker game and Levinsky knew Kreiglitz wasn't bluffing when he said he wouldn't accept disorderly conduct. And, in truth, there were no extenuating circumstances in the case. Davis was guilty of far more than a misdemeanor. Levinsky was lucky Kreiglitz was even willing to give the man that. So without pushing his luck further, Levinsky walked over to Davis and explained to him what terms Kreiglitz wanted: "Petty larceny, restitution and a fine."

Davis's jaw dropped as though he—an innocent lamb—had just been told he was going to the gas chamber. "Fine? I can't pay no fine."

"Look," Levinsky said, "you've been here before. They can bang you two-to-five. Either you pay or you sit."

For a moment, Davis's eyes clouded over at the thought of two-to-five years doing time. Then he shook his head with defeat as he accepted the idea that somehow, some way, he was going to have to come up with the money—even if he had to steal it. "Shit," he muttered.

Levinsky turned to Kreiglitz and nodded to indicate that a bargain had been struck.

Kreiglitz went over to Judge Box. "Your honor, after consulting with the defense attorney, the People are prepared to offer a reduced charge of petty larceny, section 155.25 of the Penal Code."

The judge accepted these terms and told Davis his fine would be six hundred dollars. Then he moved on to the next case, which also happened to be Levinsky's, as the back door to the court opened and three elegantly dressed people walked in.

The spectators went quiet for a time as they looked at Arthur and Rose Kirk and Clarence Middleton walk toward them. Even the lawyers in the court and some of the prisoners glanced over at the newcomers, all of whom appeared glaringly out of place in the courtroom.

Arthur and Rose Kirk were a handsome couple in their sixties. They could have entered any suburban country club in America without causing a single eyebrow to be raised, but they were as conspicuous in this courtroom as they would have been entering a strip joint on Forty-second Street. Rich, refined, well-dressed people just didn't turn up in high-crime district arraignment courts and no one knew quite what to make of them.

Arthur Kirk was a large, self-assured man who carried himself with the purposefulness of someone used to giving orders. He had a wide face with a strong, well-defined jaw that added to his look of confidence. His wife, on the other hand, seemed nervous about her surroundings. She was a pretty woman, more tasteful than stylish in appearance, with smooth, white hair and gentle, sad eyes. Her fingers twisted a beautiful pearl necklace that dangled on her neck as she followed her husband into a row of spectators.

Clarence Middleton, one of the city's foremost attorneys, had a flashier style than the Kirks. The suit he wore was obviously expensive and each accessory he had—from his shirt and shoes to his briefcase and watch—made a statement that here was a man who not only had made good but was living even better. With the demeanor of one who valued not only himself but each moment of his time, he quickly signaled the other people in the aisle to move aside and gave Arthur Kirk a glance that indicated his personal condolences for making the Kirks sit among their inferiors. Then he swiftly strolled down the center aisle of the court toward the bench.

Rose Kirk tightly squeezed a bottle of tranquilizers that she held hidden in one palm, and immediately began searching with anxious eyes among the long row of prisoners until she finally found the person she was looking for: her daughter, Claudia Draper.

For a second, the two women's eyes met. Rose Kirk looked at her daughter with a sad, beseeching gaze, but Claudia's eyes remained a blank, and just as Rose started to raise her fingers to wave, Claudia let her head drop forward, as though she had never seen Rose before in her life.

Taking her husband's hand, Rose whispered, "There she is, Arthur. She looks terrible."

Arthur Kirk patted Rose reassuringly. "Be calm," he whispered back. "Everything's under control. We'll be out of here in no time."

Meanwhile, Judge Box was proceeding with the next case. The defendant, a slender man named Gonzales, was a client of Levinsky's, but Levinsky couldn't stay focused on whatever the judge was saying to Gonzales. Instead, he watched Clarence Middleton with both disbelief and fascination. What was a big shot like Middleton doing in arraignment court? Middleton had never made an appearance there before.

Levinsky nudged Kreiglitz as Middleton opened his briefcase at a table. "Saul," Levinsky muttered, "look who's here at two hundred fifty dollars an hour. Clarence fucking Middleton."

Kreiglitz, who, like Levinsky, made a masochistic point of finding out the salaries of the city's highest-paid lawyers, shook his head and said, "Last I heard it was three-hundred-fifty."

Judge Box—perhaps the only person in the courtroom who had not seemed to take notice of Middleton and the Kirks—gave Levinsky and Kreiglitz a disapproving look for their obvious lack of interest in the Gonzales case, then turned his attention to the defendant. "Now sir," he said, "did you take property from premises at 540 East Eighth Street without permission of authority? And are you pleading guilty because you are in fact guilty and for no other reason? Say it aloud."

Gonzales glanced at Levinsky, who was still eyeing Middleton. Then he turned back to the bench and said. "I'm guilty."

Levinsky looked at the long row of prisoners, then back to Middleton, who was removing a folder from his case. "I wonder who his client is," he whispered to Kreiglitz. But Kreiglitz, feeling Judge Box's disapproval, only shrugged.

"Mr. Gonzales," the judge said, "this is your third appearance before this court in the past year. Remand for trial, April fifteen." And then, with a sarcastic edge in his voice, he added, "Thank you, Mr. Levinsky. Next case."

Levinsky looked away from Middleton long enough to see Gonzales being led off by the courtroom guard. "Sorry kid," he called out.

Gonzales rolled his eyes. "Yeah," he muttered.

Suddenly, the side door to the courtroom banged open and in walked Kreiglitz's boss from the district attorney's office, a serious-looking man in his fifties named Frank Macmillan.

Kreiglitz immediately began straightening his tie as MacMillan approached him.

"Saul," MacMillan said in an urgent, quiet voice. "Do you have the Kirk folder? I'll be taking this case."

Kreiglitz looked surprised but dug through his stack of folders until he came to one marked *Kirk, Claudia.* He handed it to MacMillan, who hurried over with it to the bench, where Clarence Middleton was already conferring in low, secretive tones with Judge Box.

Levinsky shot Kreiglitz a what-the-hell-is-going-on-here glance, but Kreiglitz only stared back at him dumbfounded. Then both men gazed up at the bench. Clarence Middleton was gesturing toward Rose and Arthur Kirk. Judge Box looked at the Kirks a moment, nodded solemnly, then whispered something to the courtroom clerk, who in turn went and whispered something to the court officer.

The officer walked over to Claudia Draper right away. "Your case is up next," he said, but Claudia ignored him and remained seated on the prisoner's bench with her head hung low. For a moment, the guard stood puzzled by her side, and then he lifted up her left arm and began to pull her toward the defendant's table.

Rose Kirk shuddered as she watched the guard

dragging her daughter across the courtroom. She hoped, at least, that Claudia might gaze up at her, but Claudia's hair swayed over her face and she continued to keep her head tucked.

"She won't look at us," Rose whispered to her husband in despair.

Arthur Kirk opened his mouth to say something comforting to Rose, but suddenly Claudia raised her head and stared at him with the same trance-like expression she had aimed at the male prisoners in the holding tanks.

Oh, you're ashamed of me now with my witch's hair in snarls and knots. You look at me as though you're still trying to find Daddy's little darling. You used to put me on your lap, brush my long curls, and say "Rapunzel, Rapunzel, let down your fair hair so that I may climb your golden stair." Well, I let down my hair. Chopped every inch of it off that night in the bathroom when I was sixteen. You and Mama stood there banging on the door, demanding to be let in as I went whack-whack-whack *at my curls until they fell onto the floor and buried me up to my ankles. You broke the lock on the door. Mama rushed in screaming when she saw me with the scissors, but you just stood there wondering where your pretty little girl had gone. Your eyes were as disappointed in me as they are now. "What have you done?" you asked. As if it weren't perfectly clear that Rapunzel had let her hair down for the very last time. . . .*

The officer pushed Claudia into her seat at the defendant's table. She sank her head down onto the cool wooden surface and ran her fingers through her hair as Arthur Kirk wiped a few drops of sweat from his face and squeezed his wife's trembling hand a little tighter.

The court clerk began reciting the facts of Claudia's case: "Calendar twenty-eight, People *versus* Claudia Kirk. The defendant is charged with murder in the first degree. Docket number 6418. Step forward and give your appearances."

Middleton smiled amiably. "Clarence Middleton for the defendant, your honor."

MacMillan gave the judge a respectful nod. "Francis Xavier Macmillan."

Levinsky, who was still standing over by Kreiglitz, suddenly broke forward. As stunned and amazed as he was by the appearance of these two men, he couldn't handle the fact that the judge was apparently breaking the rules of the courtroom for them, and was pushing aside Levinsky's next case so these two hotshots could zip in and out of the court. "Excuse me, your honor," he began, "but the Morales case is next on the docket and—"

The judge raised a hand to silence Levinsky. "All in good time, Mr. Levinsky."

But Levinsky couldn't keep his mouth shut. It had been enough having Seymour Cohen get the last word in from his limousine this morning. Levinsky's pride just couldn't take having his case pushed aside for a couple of high-rolling lawyers. "I have an appointment in part thirty, your honor," he said—hoping he sounded like a man whose time mattered.

The judge looked at Levinsky as if he were a teacher whose patience was being tried by a pesty schoolboy who wouldn't stop asking to go to the bathroom. "It'll wait, Mr. Levinsky," he said, calmly but significantly. "Sit down, please. Let's move it."

Levinsky remained standing a moment longer, looked at his watch, then went over to the public defenders' table where Kreiglitz was already seated and slammed himself down into a chair.

"Take it easy, Aaron," Kreiglitz whispered. "Watch how the big boys work. Maybe you'll learn something."

Every bone in Levinsky's body felt like grabbing Kreiglitz by the neck and strangling him. Didn't Krieglitz understand that the two of them were being treated like nothings, like fools? And why? Because in the eyes of the world they *were* nothings, *were* fools. Anyone who had more money than they did mattered more.

Levinsky threw his folders down onto the table and began doing some work. He would be damned if he'd even glance up once during the Claudia Kirk case. Let everyone else sit and *ooh* and *aah* over Middleton and MacMillan's flashy F. Lee Bailey styles. He would ignore them entirely.

Meanwhile, Clarence Middleton was striding smoothly over to Claudia. He looked at her with sympathy, and when he reached her his voice was very soft as he said, "How are you, dear?"

Claudia raised her head slowly from the table and said in a gruff, strange voice, "They've got my name wrong."

Middleton patted her hand as though she were a very small child. "We'll take care of it."

As Middleton continued to comfort Claudia, MacMillan proceeded with the case: "Your honor, the defendant, Claudia Kirk, has been indicted in the county of New York for manslaughter in the first degree."

Suddenly, Claudia snatched her hand away from Middleton and looked at the judge. "Please," she called out, "may I say something?"

Against his own intentions, Levinsky glanced up at Claudia. Middleton was obviously annoyed with her outburst and was raising a finger to his lips to silence her. Levinsky grinned to himself, pleased to see that even Clarence Middleton didn't have an easy time dealing with nut cases, and went back to his work.

MacMillan continued: "People requested that she be given psychiatric evaluation to determine her capacity to stand trial. In accordance with Article 730 of the CPL, the defendant was remanded to New York County Prison Hospital for evaluation and—"

Again, Claudia interrupted. "Excuse me?" she shouted over to the judge.

Judge Box didn't even look her way. MacMillan glanced at her from the corner of his eye, then walked up to the judge, handed the judge her folder, and began whispering and gesturing. Soon, Middleton also went toward the bench and joined in the whispering.

Claudia looked from her attorney to the judge and cupped her bandaged hand against one ear in an effort to hear what was being said.

MacMillan was speaking as low as possible. "Your honor, the psychiatrists' reports are here. They find the defendant not presently competent for trial. They recommend instead that she be committed to a mental facility. The People concur."

Again, Claudia called out: "I can't hear you! I have a right to hear you!"

Levinsky started to chuckle and gave up trying to do his work. He looked at Claudia, who was staring through her snarled mass of hair at the judge. Her eyes, which had looked so empty when he first had seen her come in the courtroom, were wild with anger and indignation.

Now she banged a hand down on her table. "I have something to say, please!"

Judge Box finally turned to her. In an extremely stern voice he said, "The defendant will keep quiet if she knows what's good for her."

Claudia slid down in her chair, but her eyes continued to focus on Judge Box with wrath.

The judge turned to Middleton. "Clarence, have you read these psychiatrists' reports?"

Middleton nodded. "I have, your honor."

"Do you move to confirm?"

"We do, your honor."

Judge Box glanced quickly at Claudia. "And have you consulted with your client?"

Middleton leaned over the bench and sighed. Letting down his attorney's mask for a moment, he said, "Larry, in view of the overriding fact—fact is, she's impossible to talk to."

But Judge Box could only stray so far from

judicial procedure. It was one thing to allow Middleton to push the Claudia Kirk case ahead on the dockets. But to have Middleton try to evade his responsibility to his client was another thing. No matter how difficult or wrong-headed a client might be, a lawyer was to be the client's advocate, and it was unethical for a lawyer to agree to the recommendations of psychiatrists in terms of placing a client in an institution without first consulting with the client. "Clarence," the judge said somberly, "please consult with your client. And make it quick."

With reluctance and obvious dread, Middleton went over to Claudia. He approached her slowly, cautiously, a kind and slightly strained smile on his face. "Claudia, dear—"

Claudia's eyes flashed with fury. "Listen," she said, "you don't have my name right. I don't want to be known as Claudia Kirk. My name is Claudia Draper."

Middleton nodded patiently. "Yes, we'll take care of that." And then, leaning close to her, speaking as gently as possible, he went on, "Now, Claudia, I'm trying to help you. We all are."

Claudia leaned back in her chair, distancing herself from Middleton, and looked around her. "What's going on here?"

"We're trying to do what we feel is best for you," Middleton said reassuringly.

Claudia jerked her head back toward Middleton and gave him a sharp glance through her mass of hair. "We?" she asked.

"We offered you criminally negligent homicide and you didn't want to—"

"Hey!" Claudia shouted. "Who are you?"

Middleton stepped away from her, a little taken aback. "What?"

Claudia's eyes became more intense. "Who *are* you?" she asked again.

"Clarence Middleton. Don't you remember?"

Levinsky, watching from the corner of his eye, had to put a hand to his mouth to keep from laughing. He could almost feel Middleton's embarrassed confusion in trying to deal with this hostile client.

"Who do you work for, Clarence?" Claudia asked.

Middleton's eyes narrowed at Claudia's use of his first name, but he recovered quickly and smiled again at her. "I'm your lawyer, Claudia."

Claudia pushed her hair back from her face. Levinsky suddenly noticed her high cheekbones. He also noticed that there was something cunning in her awareness of Middleton's condescension. "Good, good," she said sweetly. "We're on the right track."

Middleton nodded. "We have to claim that you're incompetent to stand trial. Do you understand?"

"I didn't give you permission to do that. I'm not incompetent," Claudia said.

"Of course you're not, dear," Middleton cooed.

"I'm *innocent*."

Middleton sighed. "I know that, but that's not the issue."

For a moment Claudia's lips began to turn up

with a strange smile. Then she brought her face back into control and said, "It's not?"

Leaning his hands down onto the table, Middleton began a patient explanation. "The doctors agree and your mother and father agree, it's best if you're in a hospital rather than in a prison. Look, Claudia, your mother and father love you. It's all been arranged."

Suddenly, Claudia bolted up from the chair. "You fucking son of a bitch!" she screamed, and hurled herself across the table at him. Like a wild animal, she tore at Middleton with her nails and teeth, striking ferociously at his face, his stomach, his head.

Middleton was so surprised at the attack that for a moment he stood frozen, defenseless. Then he tried to protect his face from Claudia's scratches. He made a move to cover his expensive, designer-frame eyeglasses, but Claudia smashed them across his face, shattering the lenses. She kicked at him as he stumbled, pounded him with a rage so startling that almost everyone in the courtroom came to their feet in horror.

Levinsky had never seen a person go so quickly out of control. His mouth dropped open as he watched Middleton curl up in pain from the force of Claudia's blows. But what shocked him most were the noises she made as she attacked. She screeched and screamed and cursed viciously.

In the back of the courtroom, Rose Kirk began to weep violently and called out, "Arthur, stop her!"

Arthur Kirk began racing toward Claudia, but by this time she had slammed Middleton across the defendant's table. He sprawled helplessly on his back, his papers flying across the courtroom, as she leaped onto his stomach. Her robe opened, her hair blew over her face, and the blows she struck echoed in the courtroom.

Judge Box stood up. Banging his gavel, he shouted, "Get her out! Get her back down! Quiet in the court!" And, as Arthur Kirk tried to pull Claudia off Middleton, "Officer, get him!"

The court officers ran frantically, trying to deal with Claudia and Arthur Kirk at once. They grabbed Claudia's arms, but she yanked herself free. Arthur Kirk was almost as hard to restrain. His face turned red with anger as he saw the force the officers were using on Claudia and he tried to shove them away from her. They, in turn, shoved him back as Claudia continued pummeling Middleton.

Finally, an officer pinned Arthur Kirk's arms to his sides. He pushed and shoved to free himself as four other officers pulled Claudia off Middleton.

"Sir!" Judge Box called out. "Restrain yourself."

Arthur Kirk turned furiously to the judge. "That's my daughter, goddamn you!"

But Judge Box didn't seem to care. "Sit down," he ordered, "or we'll have to remove you."

Arthur Kirk turned to Claudia with agonized eyes as he watched the officers lift her up, kicking and screaming and start carrying her toward the courtroom doors. For a few seconds, he seemed to consider running after her, forcing the officers to put her down, but then he let himself be led back to his seat.

Claudia was still screaming and struggling. As the officers lifted her past one corner of the room, she even grabbed down the New York State flag and began beating them with it. One of the officers tried to pry her fingers from it and she bit him.

Her face was purple with rage. She hurled the flag this way and that, as though she were intent on striking out at every person in the courtroom. The spectators stood at attention, some terrified, most merely fascinated and vastly entertained.

Levinsky watched as the officers finally managed to remove the flag from her hands, and half dragged, half lifted her out of the courtroom. He could hear her screaming even as the doors closed behind her.

Slowly, everyone in the courtroom turned toward Middleton. The once-elegant lawyer was bleeding, his glasses were punched apart, and his expensive suit was ripped to shreds.

MacMillan went over to Middleton and helped him off the table. "Are you all right, Clarence?"

Middleton stared around him, as though he couldn't quite accept the fact that he, Clarence Middleton, had just been made to suffer. At last he touched a hand to his face, felt a cut at his eyebrow, then looked at the blood and whispered, "I'm bleeding . . . my glasses."

A few of the more hard-hearted spectators

laughed at Middleton's concern over his glasses. He should have been concerned about whether he would ever be able to walk again.

Levinsky felt numb. All of his jealousy for Middleton's high-powered career slid away when he saw how vulnerable the man had suddenly become. It wasn't so much that Levinsky was experiencing even the slightest change of heart about wishing he had Middleton's money and power. But he was stunned to see that even those with money and power could be spat on by the gods. And if such things could happen to a man like Middleton, didn't it follow that even worse things could happen to Levinsky?

Judge Box banged his gavel a few more times and then looked over at Middleton. He waited a respectful moment or two for the attorney to compose himself, then calmly said, "Can we go on?"

Middleton stared at the judge aghast. "No, we can't go on!" he cried out. "I've been attacked in a courtroom, for chrissake. I hereby request to be removed from this case."

But Judge Box pressed on despite Middleton's outrage. "Can't you just move to confirm?"

"No sir!" Middleton said indignantly. "Get someone from Legal Aid. I've got to get to a doctor."

And with that Middleton turned and hobbled out of the courtroom, dragging his expensive briefcase behind him.

The judge didn't miss a beat. Putting the entire ordeal of Claudia and Middleton behind him, he smoothed his robes, sat down, and looked around the courtroom. "Do we have a Legal Aid member?"

A sick feeling began to come over Levinsky.

The judge turned to his bridgeman. "Where's Torbick? Where's Morella? Is there anyone here on the appointments list?"

No, Levinsky thought. Oh God, no!

Levinsky grabbed his stack of folders and began rushing toward the side door. If he could only make it out into the corridor before being spotted by Judge Box! If just this one time in life he could have a single, solitary touch of good luck!

But the judge roared out his name: *"Levinsky!"*

Levinsky stopped cold and froze.

"Levinsky," the judge went on, "where are you going?"

Ruefully, Levinsky turned around. With a sheepish look on his face, he said, "To get Morella." And then, as a last, desperate ploy: "Your honor, I've got an appearance in part thirty. Let me get Morella. Morella's on catch."

The judge merely grinned. "But I've caught *you.*"

"Your honor," Levinsky begged, "I respectfully submit that my caseload—"

"Mr. Levinsky," the judge said severely. "Perhaps your caseload is too heavy to accept any appointments from this court?"

Levinsky fumed but said nothing. That's right, he thought, give me the choice of either defending Ms. Godzilla or watching my family starve to death. Such wonderful free choices are open to us here in America . . .

The judge turned to the court recorder. "For the record, Mr. Middleton withdraws and Mr. Levinsky is appointed for the defense."

Like a condemned man, Levinsky slowly approached the bench. MacMillan was waiting for him with the folder for Claudia's case.

"It's a 730," Macmillan said kindly. "We have two psychiatric reports on her and a motion from the defense to confirm. Just take a move."

Levinsky knew what he was supposed to do next. He was to agree that Claudia should be placed in an institution. The move he was to make was to confirm. But something went hard in him and he just couldn't make the motion—not after being jerked around by Judge Box.

He looked at the judge. He knew that the one thing Box couldn't bear was a delay, and proudly said, "I haven't seen the reports."

MacMillan shrugged to Judge Box. Years back, before MacMillan had been promoted, he had battled cases against Levinsky and knew Levinsky's peculiar brand of ethics, which seemed to MacMillan to be more about bullheaded stubbornness than true liberal idealism.

Judge Box glared at Levinsky. Pointing to the reports, he said, "So see them." And he shoved the reports across the bench.

Levinsky picked up the reports and began glancing through them. He read some of the phrases the psychiatrists had used to describe Claudia:

"paranoid," "erratic," "deeply disturbed," "poor impulse control," "hysterical," "extremely hostile," and so forth. All the phrases seemed to him to be gross understatements.

The judge was eager to get his court back on schedule. "Let's move it," he said. "Let's get this one out of here."

Levinsky ignored the judge. "What's the original charge?" he asked.

The judge rolled his eyes, but MacMillan said, "Manslaughter."

"The original charge is not the issue," the judge said coolly. "Psychiatrists' reports say she's unfit to stand trial. Let's have your motion."

But Levinsky kept his mouth closed and went back to reading the reports.

Judge Box sighed. "Didn't you say you were in a *hurry*, Mr. Levinsky?"

"I *am* in a hurry," Levinsky said.

"Then let's have your motion. I don't have all day."

Levinsky slammed down the reports on Claudia and stared at Judge Box, who stared right back at him. For a time, the two men looked at each other like gunslingers who were meeting at high noon for a shoot-out. Then Levinsky calmly said, "I move to controvert."

Judge Box appeared not only angry, but shocked. To controvert was to oppose the psychiatrists' recommendations and to claim that Claudia was fit to stand trial.

Every lawyer in the courtroom was surprised by

Levinsky's stance. Kreiglitz shook his head sadly at his friend's self-destructive nature. He knew Levinsky just couldn't bear being at the mercy of Judge Box, but to go and controvert was altogether too much. Everyone over the age of two in the courtroom had just seen that the defendant was not only unfit to stand trial but was unfit to be allowed out of a padded cell without a straitjacket.

"You wanted a motion?" Levinsky asked casually. "That's my motion."

Kreiglitz sighed.

"What's your basis, Levinsky?" MacMillan asked.

"Your honor, the defendant, as I observed, seemed a bit reluctant. I have to consult with my client."

The judge tried to hold back his anger. "Fine," he said. "I'll see you tomorrow."

Levinsky's eyes widened. This he hadn't expected. "Tomorrow? I've got cases tomorrow."

Judge Box turned to his clerk. "Continue to tomorrow," he said blandly. "Calendar one. Now we'll proceed."

For a moment, Levinsky thought of begging the judge for one more day, but then he realized he would never be given it, so instead he just spun around from the bench and stormed out of the courtroom.

Kreiglitz followed swiftly on Levinsky's heels but still had to run to catch up to him in the corridor. Levinsky was pushing past people, trying to put as much distance as possible between himself and Judge Box.

Finally, Kreiglitz caught up with his friend. "Are you out of your mind?" he asked.

Levinsky's eyes flashed with self-righteous conviction. "I don't have to take that shit from him."

Kreiglitz shook his head. "Of course you do. He's the judge."

Levinsky considered this for a moment, but said nothing.

"Look, do yourself a favor," Kreiglitz went on. "Go back in there and settle up."

But Levinsky was too far gone to be wise. His pride was at stake. To hell with the fact that what he was doing was stupid. Ignoring Kreiglitz's advice, he merely smiled and said, "Jesus! Did you see that girl work over Middleton?"

Kreiglitz laughed in spite of himself. "I wish she woulda nailed MacMillan, too," he admitted.

Suddenly, Levinsky felt a tap on his shoulder. "Pardon me, Mr. Levinsky?"

Levinsky turned and saw himself face-to-face with the large, powerful man who had identified himself as Claudia's father in the courtroom. He was standing with his arm wrapped protectively around his wife.

"I'd like to talk to you," Arthur Kirk said.

Kreiglitz began to back away. "I'll see you later, Aaron," he said, and took off for the courtroom.

Levinsky stared at the respectable couple before him. How had they managed to raise a monster like Claudia? Of course, the father did seem to be able to put up a good fight. But the woman appeared so timid, so refined, that it was hard to believe she and Claudia were related.

Arthur Kirk extended his right hand by way of introduction. "I'm Arthur Kirk," he said. "I'm the girl's father. This is my wife Rose."

Levinsky shook hands with the Kirks. "Hello."

Arthur Kirk sighed. "I'm still shaking," he said, "I can't believe what went on in there." And then, suddenly becoming quite earnest: "Why did you stop the motion?"

Because I'm a jerk, Levinsky thought. But out loud, he said, "I'm not familiar with the case yet."

Arthur Kirk's eyes seemed to deepen in color. "The case," he said firmly, "is about a very disturbed girl, isn't that clear? She needs to be hospitalized."

Levinsky looked at the floor. "I have to read the reports," he said. "I have to confer with the defendent."

Arthur Kirk suddenly raised his voice: "How can you confer? She's sick; she's not in her right mind. You can see that!"

At first, Levinsky started to feel his shoulders sag under the weight of Arthur Kirk's words. Truly, the behavior of Claudia in the courtroom had not inspired much confidence in Levinsky about her sanity. Maybe he should return to the judge while he could, beg forgiveness for his rash behavior the way Kreiglitz had suggested, and spare this family a lot of needless suffering.

Levinsky looked up from the floor and opened his mouth to tell Arthur Kirk that he would go back to Judge Box and put forward a motion to confirm the psychiatrist's findings. But then he found himself remembering how ardently Claudia had screamed out the words "I am not incompetent," and something deep inside him made him go silent.

What to do? Well, he knew what Kreiglitz wanted him to do. He knew what Judge Box wanted him to do. He knew what these concerned parents wanted him to do. But he couldn't do it. The schlemiel in him was intent on at least interviewing Claudia and reading over the reports before letting her be locked up. And so, knowing he was being a weak-kneed liberal, a joke, he looked into Arthur Kirk's angry eyes and said, "I'm sorry about your daughter, sir, I know it's painful for you."

Arthur Kirk's nostrils flared. "You're damn right it's painful. What about *her* pain?"

Rose Kirk stepped forward and squeezed her husband's arm in a soothing manner. Gently, trying to calm him, she whispered, "Arthur . . ."

But Arthur Kirk had no intention of being calmed down. "We're talking about my child. She needs to be in a hospital, not in some prison cell. She's in no condition to stand trial."

"Darling," Rose Kirk said quietly, "he didn't say he wouldn't do it."

Rose Kirk's logic seemed to have an immediate effect on her husband. The anger in his eyes was replaced with hopefulness. He even looked a bit apologetic as he said, "Of course you didn't say that, did you?"

Levinsky stood silent.

"Please forgive me," Arthur Kirk went on. "I'm not handling this well."

"It's perfectly understandable, Mr. Kirk," Levinsky said.

Now Rose Kirk stepped forward. Nervously, with her voice breaking, she said, "Will you be going to see her?"

Levinsky almost grimaced. The thought of having a comfy little chat with the Kirks' daughter over in the psychiatric section of the New York County Prison Hospital was not exactly thrilling to him. He looked forward to talking to Claudia about as much as he looked forward to dying. But he kept his tone professional as he said, "I will have to see her, yes."

Rose Kirk's lips trembled. Levinsky thought she might break down and cry but she squared her shoulders and said, "Will you tell her I love her?"

"I will," Levinsky said. But he wondered how easy it was to tell someone her mother loves her when she is chasing you around with a New York State flag aimed as a dagger at your heart. God, he hoped there weren't any flags hanging at the prison hospital.

Rose Kirk leaned forward, her eyes brimming with tears. "Please," she said.

Meanwhile, Arthur Kirk was removing his wallet. He handed Levinsky a card as though the two of them were executives meeting at a sales conference. "If you need anything, Mr. Levinsky, anything at all, call my office. Here's my card."

Levinsky took the rich, cream-colored card and shoved it into his pants pocket without looking at it. "Thanks," he said.

Rose Kirk stared at Levinsky with her sad eyes. Although Levinsky pitied her, he felt uncomfortable having to be so close to someone whose pain he was partially causing. He began to back away from both of the Kirks with a nod of his head.

And then he was off, rushing down the corridor to a rickety staircase that would lead him to his next appointment of the day. He tore up the steps two at a time, unaware that he was moving as quickly and forcefully as the successful men he had watched from his escalator earlier this morning. He thought only that he had been right to believe today was going to be rotten to the core. He had no idea how he was going to manage to make it through all his regular work, let alone find the time to review Claudia's file.

And then there was the matter of actually having to talk with Claudia. If she turned out to be as crazy as everyone insisted she was, he would have to tell her that he was going to recommend institutionalization, just as Middleton had. And Levinsky, after seeing what Claudia had done to Middleton, was not too eager to see what she would then do to him. Spear him with a flagpole, perhaps?

TWO

At eight o'clock that night, Levinsky bought himself a package of Rolaids for dinner and began to trudge over to the New York County Prison Hospital for his meeting with Claudia. He read the reports on her as he walked, pausing beneath street lamps and neon signs when the sky grew too dark for him to make out the spidery handwriting of the psychiatrists who had interviewed her during her confinement at the hospital.

All around Levinsky, men and women who had spent their days in gray suits and starched white shirts were emerging from apartment buildings like butterflies set free from their cocoons. Men who in daylight tried their best to blend in were now trying their best to stand out. In bright pullovers and baggy cotton pants, they hurried along the streets in pursuit of women who wore shimmering blouses and swaying pastel skirts. Levinsky could smell a thousand after-shaves and a thousand perfumes rush by him, but none of the smells or sights around him registered. He was lost in the world of Claudia's past, and the present world was only a blur as he walked slower and slower, becoming more and more mystified by the woman he would be defending in court the next day.

According to the history the psychiatrists had prepared about her, Claudia had once been the sort of daughter people like Arthur and Rose Kirk would have raised. She had grown up in a wealthy suburb of Long Island, gone to a prestigious college, married a successful businessman, and moved with him to an even wealthier suburb than the one in which she had grown up. There she had proceeded to be a model housewife for some years. So far, so good. But one day, she walked out the door on her husband and rented an apartment in Manhattan. This was where things began to get murky in her life, and where she had ceased to give information to her psychiatrists, but somewhere along the line, following her divorce, she had drifted into a life of prostitution. Why? When the psychiatrists had questioned her, she had replied, "Why not?"

Both of the psychiatrists who had interviewed Claudia believed she had lost her mind—and not merely her morals—around the time of her divorce. The psychiatrists believed she had suffered a collapse of some kind from which she had yet to recover, a collapse which had left her paranoid, dangerous to herself and others, and frighteningly hostile toward men. They recommended that she undergo intense psychotherapy before being brought to trial.

Levinsky wished he had had a chance to read the reports before going against the findings of the doctors. Just how the hell was he suppposed to prove that someone could go from being the perfect wife to the killer call girl *without* being nuts?

He sighed and closed the reports. Ahead of him loomed the New York County Prison Hospital. It was an enormous brown brick building, built back in the 1800s and never fully renovated since that time. The windows were narrowed and either boarded up or heavily barred. A huge barbed-wire fence enclosed the grounds, which gave the place a menacing, nightmarish quality.

Levinsky dreaded going in the hospital, but after popping two more Rolaids into his mouth, he walked up to the guard at the doors, showed his identification, and entered.

A sign in the dank, light green lobby read PSYCHIATRIC DIVISION—FOLLOW RED LINE. Levinsky looked down at the floor. Red, white, blue, yellow and green lines formed a mad maze beneath his feet. He tried to follow the red line as best as he could, but it kept leading him into corners. He felt like a laboratory rat in search of cheese that some scientist didn't want him to find.

Finally, Levinsky gave up on the red line entirely and wandered over to a soft-drink machine. Forgetting that today was not his day for dealing with vending machines, he tried to get himself a Pepsi. No go. Furious with the machine, the red lines, and especially with himself, he began to beat the machine mercilessly.

A nurse walked by and gave him the kind of sharp, disapproving look that made Levinsky suddenly think of his wife, whom he had yet to call and inform that he would be getting home at God-knows-what hour. Not that his wife actually worried about him when he didn't get home at a reasonable hour, but she would be sure to pick a fight about his absolute lack of consideration.

Levinsky gave the machine one more whack as a gesture of defiance against both his wife and the nurse and then walked on, his hands sore, his conscience vaguely troubled. He probably did lack consideration, not only for his wife, but for his new client as well. What favors would he be doing this crazed woman by going along with her demented dreams of proving herself competent to stand trial for manslaughter? Wasn't she much better off, as her father had suggested, getting treatment in this hospital than in going through a taxing and draining sanity hearing? And suppose he managed to get her declared sane and she had to stand trial? What jury would vote her innocent of manslaughter if she turned violent on them in the courtroom and began chasing them about with flagpoles?

Levinsky walked over to an orderly and asked for directions to the psychiatric wing. The orderly didn't even look up from a floor he was mopping, but merely grunted, "Follow the red line."

Reluctantly, Levinsky turned his eyes back to the

ground and continued following the red line into dead ends. But eventually, almost miraculously, he stumbled upon the wing.

The admitting area was a soft, sanity-inducing beige. There was a huge barred door, equipped with a big lock, and a kind of caged area where an attendant sat. Levinsky walked up to the cage and was about to show his identification and ask for Claudia when the barred door opened and a man appeared.

Ignoring Levinsky, the attendant in the cage called out, "Good night, Dr. Morrison."

Dr. Morrison, a middle-aged man with an air of self-importance that Levinsky instantly resented, turned to the attendant with a kind of noblesse-oblige smile on his face and said, "Good night, John."

Levinsky opened his mouth to talk with the attendant, then suddenly recalled that Dr. Morrison was one of the two psychiatrists who had written about Claudia in the reports Levinsky had read.

Levinsky spun toward the man. "Excuse me? Dr. Morrison?"

Dr. Morrison turned and looked at Levinsky with impatience. "Yes?"

Levinsky walked over to him. "I read the report from you and Dr. Arantes on Claudia Draper. My name's Levinsky. I'm her attorney.

The doctor eyed Levinsky suspiciously. "Is there going to be a hearing on this matter?"

Levinsky shrugged. "Could be," he said. "You got a minute?"

Dr. Morrison's eyes narrowed. "Not about Mrs. Draper," he said firmly. "I'm not sure that would be ethical. Sorry." And with that he walked off.

Flipping open the report on Claudia to the pages Morrison had written, Levinsky chased after the man. "I'm just curious about a couple of things," he called out. "You say she was flagrantly sexual, subject to random visions, paranoid—"

Dr. Morrison cut Levinsky off without stopping: "I'm *really* sorry, Mr. Levinsky."

But Levinsky stayed on the man's heels. He was used to being treated with indifference bordering on contempt. The reward of having no pride in himself was that he didn't have to worry about feeling humiliated. So he pressed on: "Look, doc, one question. Is she crazy?"

Suddenly, Morrison came to a dead stop. Levinsky almost tripped over the man as Dr. Morrison spun around and said, "*Crazy* is a word I dislike. Do I think she should go to a prison? No. She is where she belongs, Mr. Levinsky. Good night." And then he walked away a final time.

Levinsky watched the doctor strut along the hallway for a moment but didn't pursue him. What was the point in trying to talk to some pretentious shrink who spent his days deciding people were crazy and his nights saying other people shouldn't even use the word?

The attendant in the caged booth was looking at Levinsky with an amused grin. Levinsky wondered why it was that minimum-wage employees always seemed to get an incredible kick out of seeing their bosses lord their power over people. You'd think the attendant would hate a creep like Morrison, but instead he respected the bastard.

Levinsky decided to ignore the attendant's sadistic glee. He walked up to him, flashed his identification, then said, "I have an appointment to see Claudia Draper."

The attendant eyed Levinsky's ID carefully, as though Levinsky was the sort of person who tried to break into mental institutions for cheap thrills, but finally nodded his head and opened the large, barred door.

Levinsky entered a strange, almost deserted corridor that was half lit and full of huge shadows. A couple of inmates wandered aimlessly about in hospital robes, drugged or out of touch with reality. They didn't even glance at Levinsky as he walked past them, but seemed to stare through him as if he were invisible.

At the end of the corridor was a large lounge. Though furnished with tables, couches, and chairs, it had a forlorn, empty appearance. Levinsky felt depressed just entering it, and wondered how people who were actually suffering from depression could ever hope to get well in such a place as this.

There were patients sitting idly on the couches. Like the patients in the corridor, they also seemed oblivious to Levinsky's presence. They sat like rag dolls in their robes, dull-eyed, sunken, closed off. Unlike Claudia, they appeared utterly passive.

Levinsky couldn't picture any of them chasing after him with a New York State flag.

"You can wait in here," the attendant said, and walked off toward another half-lit corridor.

Levinsky stood uncomfortably in a corner of the room. He eyed the patients around him and wondered if he was looking at Dr. Morrison's failures or successes. Was the point of being institutionalized to become so placid that you no longer reacted to life? He thought of Claudia's overreaction to life and considered whether she would be more fit to stand trial if she became one of these couch potatoes.

In a moment the attendant was back again, but not with Claudia. He came over to Levinsky and said, "Dr. Arantes thought you'd prefer to be alone with Mrs. Draper during your meeting, so I've been told to take you to the conference room."

Levinsky followed the attendant to a tiny room that contained a single table. Levinsky looked at it and shuddered as he pictured Claudia hurling him across it, beating him worse than she had beaten Middleton.

"I'll be back in a minute with Mrs. Draper," the attendant said. Then he closed the door behind him, leaving Levinsky alone with his fears.

Levinsky sat down at the table and drummed his fingers anxiously across it. Being alone with Claudia in this stuffy, cramped room was not exactly a happy prospect. At least in the lounge, there were places to run and hide if she turned violent on him. But what was to become of him in here? Yes, he could dive under the table if she came after him, but suppose she knocked him unconscious before he could scream for help?

With a sigh, Levinsky popped another Rolaids in his mouth, glanced up at the door, and began to prepare for the worst.

For hours, Claudia had been tied to her bed, spread-eagled, her arms and legs wrapped with canvas restraints that were fastened to each of her bedposts. Her hair hung over her face, and beads of sweat dripped from her forehead, through her mass of hair, and down her neck. She seemed oblivious to her own sweat as she stared at the ceiling.

A nurse entered her room and began to untie one of Claudia's wrists. Claudia looked from the corner of her eye at the nurse's hand, but said nothing.

The door to Claudia's room opened again to admit Dr. Arantes, a thick-featured South American with greased black hair. Immediately, Claudia turned her eyes back to the ceiling.

Dr. Arantes put his hands into the deep pockets of his white coat and watched as the nurse set Claudia's right arm free, then he walked to the side of Claudia's bed and spoke to her in an accent so deep his words were almost indecipherable. "How 'ees eet wit choo, Claudia? Choo feel better? Choo feel more calm?"

Claudia acted as though she couldn't hear him.

Dr. Arantes came closer to her face. He watched

the sweat drip from her neck to her breasts. "Choo are a woman of passion and passion ees not good here. Passion in the bedroom ees good. But not here."

The nurse glanced over at the doctor for permission to remove the other restraints, but for a time the doctor ignored her as he looked fixedly at the beads of sweat gliding over Claudia's body. Then he merely nodded his permission to the nurse and walked to the foot of Claudia's bed, where his gaze lingered for some moments on the space between her bound legs, before he finally turned away and said, "Someone is wait for to see you."

Freed from her restraints, Claudia sat up and slowly climbed out of her bed. Dr. Arantes walked out into the corridor and signaled the nurse to bring Claudia after him. Claudia followed the doctor, staring numbly at his white coat.

That white coat against his slicked hair. The maître d' at the Walnut Room—that's who he looks like. Only the maître d's white coat was cleaner and his hair was much thicker. I followed him as he led me into the restaurant. "This way, Mrs. Draper," he said. "Ah, thank you, Manuel," I replied. I walked slowly, my hips swaying to the piano music playing softly across the room. Good old Manuel, always such a proper gentleman, so well mannered and formal, and so very understanding so long as I slipped him a twenty. He led me to my table. And that was where I saw good old "Allen Green" for the first time. He was sitting there with his anxious-eyed face, and his hot-night-in-the-big-

city suit. A fifty-year-old man who probably hadn't gotten laid in ten years. He stood up for his four-hundred-dollar lady, his eyes popping out at me almost as far as his pants. "You must be Claudia," he said. And I smiled breathlessly, as though I was seeing Clark Gable instead of a very tired businessman. "I do hope you're Mr. Green from Chicago." His face turned red. Their faces always turned red when I used their fake names. "Call me Allen," he said. And then he asked me if I wanted champagne. I thanked him with such sincerity, my eyes starting to look him over. He sat there fumbling with his napkin while I checked him out. "I've never had to take a test before," he said, "not since school anyway. What do you think?" What did I think? I thought he looked like a lot of men I'd had, men whose wives had turned cold without their ever knowing why. He glanced at me nervously and pulled at imaginary lint on his jacket. Could he even remember a time before his wife began to have kids and headaches. "Maybe a little too much waist?" he asked. "Nice suit, though, don't you think?" I thought his suit looked wrinkled from a long flight in a stuffed overnight bag. But I let my tongue flick across my lips and I whispered, "You look fine, Allen. Don't take it personally. It's just the way I do things." I stared into his eyes, thinking I was so smart I knew all about him from the eyes. "Blue eyes," I cooed. "He grinned. "Twenty-twenty. Hundred and seventy-five pounds, six-foot-one. No major illnesses." I leaned close and whispered, "They did a study on blue eyes. They found out blue-eyed men make the best quarterbacks and financial wizards." And then I looked deep, deep, deep into his weary eyes and said, "I think they make the best lovers." He was really getting turned on. "Do you have certain questions that you ask? That sort of thing?" he asked. "No," I said, "I just go by the seat of my pants." He looked at me with need: "Well, how am I doing?" I said, "I'm about to slide off my chair." Oh, and did that ever make his tired eyes dance and his nervous smile grow. Gulping, he turned to the waiter and yelled, "Check please!"

Suddenly, the attendant walked up to Dr. Arantes and the nurse, whispered something to them, then approached Claudia. He took Claudia by the arm and led her toward the conference room as Dr. Arantes and the nurse walked off in the opposite direction.

As soon as the attendant opened the door to the room, Claudia yanked away from his grasp. The attendant pushed her into the room and, without a word, closed the door quickly, leaving Levinsky to deal with Claudia entirely on his own.

Levinsky rose nervously from the table. "Hello, Mrs. Draper."

Claudia glared at him by way of response.

Levinsky swallowed and smiled at her in much the same way that a mailman might smile at a rabid dog. "My name's Aaron Levinsky," he said soothingly.

Claudia continued to glare.

Levinsky reached into his pocket and offered her his business card as a kind of doggy bone. "I'm a lawyer," he said slowly and calmly. "I've been sent here by the court. Mr. Middleton doesn't represent you anymore."

Claudia's glare deepened.

Levinsky plodded on. "Would you like to discuss your case with me?"

Claudia's glare deepened even more.

For a moment, Levinsky considered rushing out the door, but then he realized that in order to do that, he'd have to walk past Claudia, which he did not particularly care to do. So instead he just gave up and sank down into his chair. Let her come for him, kick him, scratch him, bite him. Anything was better than anticipating what was to come. "Look," he said wearily, "I don't know if you can follow this but I gotta go to court tomorrow on your behalf and tonight I gotta go home to Queens on the subway, which, by the way, scares the shit outta me. I'm tired, I feel a little sick, and it's been a long day."

Claudia took a step forward. Now it's coming, Levinsky thought. Now I'm really gonna get it. Tomorrow's headlines will read: POVERTY-STRICKEN JEWISH LAWYER FOUND DEAD IN LOONY BIN—WIFE BITTER BECAUSE THE BUM DIDN'T EVEN HAVE LIFE INSURANCE. But instead of attacking Levinsky, Claudia merely said, "I can follow that."

Levinsky glanced sharply at her. The hostile gleam was gone. In its place was a slyly sarcastic glint.

Levinsky was unable to resist the dare of this new look. Dangerous Claudia might be, but if she thought she could outdo him in the realm of being a smart aleck, she had another think coming. "Ah, terrific!" he said, "You can talk!"

Claudia snorted. "Talk, dance, card tricks, juggle. What kind of show do I have to put on for you?"

Levinsky pulled back. Maybe he had gone too far. Not wanting to incur her wrath, he said, "Did I say something wrong?"

Claudia approached him angrily. "Well," she said, "I won't get a fair trial unless I put on a good show for—who now?" And she finally looked at his business card: "Aaron Levinsky, Legal Aid."

Levinsky shook his head nervously. "No, no," he said, "it's not like that—"

Claudia cut him off. "No? How *do* I get a fair trial?"

"It has nothing to do—"

Slamming her hand down on the table, Claudia exploded: *"How do I get to stand trial? That's what I want to know!"*

Suddenly, the door opened. The attendant walked in quickly and looked at Levinsky questioningly.

Levinsky turned from the attendant to Claudia's furious face and back again. Should he just get the hell out now? Leave before she made mincemeat out of him? Yes, yes he should! But when the attendant started for Claudia, Levinsky found himself putting his hand up and saying, "It's all right. I'm her lawyer."

"Says who?" Claudia sneered.

"Says the court," Levinsky said firmly.

The attendant shrugged. "Well, if you need me, give me a holler." And he left.

Levinsky eyed Claudia a moment. "Do you think I'll need him?"

Claudia smiled bitterly. "Haven't you heard? I lash out and strike people at random."

"I know," Levinsky said. "I was there. I think you broke his nose."

Flopping herself down in a chair, Claudia said, "So the day's not a total loss."

Levinsky laughed. The woman might be crazy, but she wasn't stupid. He grinned as he laid his briefcase out and began to get to work. "So," he said, removing a folder from his case, "what we've got here is a 730 process, a process whereby—"

"You married?" Claudia asked.

Levinsky glanced up from his folder. "What?"

Claudia smiled. "You got a missus?"

"Yes."

Claudia opened her eyes wide and pleasantly asked, "Does she give good head?"

Instantly, Levinsky's face went red and he almost dropped the folder on the floor. He collected himself quickly but saw that Claudia had picked up on his embarrassment and he felt annoyed both with her and himself. "Look," he said, "you want to talk about your situation here? You've been indicted for manslaughter, first degree."

"I know all that," Claudia said. And then she leaned toward Levinsky and looked into his eyes. "Tell me why you're really here."

Levinsky, still strung out from Claudia's question about his wife, was befuddled. Why *was* he really here? He frowned. "The truth?"

Claudia rolled her eyes with disgust. "No, Levinsky, the bullshit. I love listening to bullshit, especially when I'm drowning in it." She stood up and paced the room with fury, then shook her head and said, "I *know* why you're here. You're here to see for yourself if I'm crazy. No, no, no! You're here to see just *how* crazy I am."

Quietly, Levinsky said, "Two psychiatrists say you're incompetent."

Claudia continued to pace the room. "Morrison and Arantes. Frick 'n Frack. Arantes can barely speak English and Morrison's a very weird guy. I flashed and he didn't even look."

Levinsky started to smile, but suddenly Claudia spun toward him and, with a single yank on the tie to her hospital gown, exposed herself to him. His mouth dropped open as he stared at her perfectly shaped breasts, her curved hips, her slender thighs. So that, he thought in amazement, is how a woman is supposed to look.

Claudia grinned mischievously as she held her gown wide. "How 'bout you, Levinsky, are you weird, too?"

His face was again a bright shade of red, but he didn't particularly care. "I must be okay," Levinsky said. "I'm looking."

Claudia laughed and retied her gown. Levinsky was watching her when she glanced up again. Their eyes met and for a second Levinsky thought she was starting to blush, too, but then she walked away from him.

"Your mother said to tell you she loves you," Levinsky said at last.

Claudia instantly turned back to him. "Fuck my mother!" she shouted. "Why didn't you tell me you were working for them?"

Levinsky sighed. "From Mr. Hyde to Dr. Jekyll and back again. "Look, lady," he began, "I came here to do my job in good faith. You can cooperate and maybe it goes your way. Or you can yell at me and tomorrow I move to commit and that's that."

"You creep lawyers are all alike," Claudia said. "As long as you get your fee, you don't care who goes where for how long."

Levinsky rolled his his eyes. His fee. Oh yeah. The millions he made.

Claudia walked toward him, pointing at his neck. "Now this one comes in," she said, "wearing the worst tie I've ever seen, and tells me that if I don't kiss ass he's going to walk out on me. Well, walk!"

Making an effort not to look down at his tie—it was a Father's Day present from one of his kids, for chrissake—Levinsky said, "And be held in contempt of court? No thank you."

Claudia shrugged.

What a bitch, Levinsky thought. As though she was doing him a favor letting him be her lawyer. But out loud he said, "You'll have to hire your own shrink to take a look at you. Then you'll have to convince him you're not incompetent."

Claudia shook her head. "Wrong. No more shrinks."

"I'm giving you good legal advice here," Levinsky said patiently.

But Claudia dismissed him with a wave of her hand. "Thank you, but you know what I said about lawyers? Goes double for shrinks."

"They got doctors saying you're crazy," Levinsky pointed out. "You need at least one doctor saying you're not crazy, or you got no case."

"Sure I do," Claudia insisted. "*I'm* my case. I get up, say my piece, prove I'm competent."

Oy vey, Levinsky thought as he tried to picture the scene: Claudia up on the witness stand trying to prove her competence by flashing Judge Box, by chasing everyone with flagpoles, and by screaming and swearing anytime somebody said something she didn't like. Sure she could prove she was competent—competent to be measured for a straitjacket.

Claudia went on heatedly. "I don't want any more quacks running around in my head, asking about my toilet training."

Levinsky smacked the table. His patience was gone. This loudmouthed hysteric thought she knew better than he did how to prove her negligible sanity. "The only thing that scares me is a stupid client," he told her. "You terrify me. Have you ever been cross-examined? Do you know what it's like?"

"No," Claudia said softly as Levinsky stood up and came toward her with angry, flashing eyes.

"How long have you been hooking?" Levinsky asked.

Claudia looked at the floor. "Three years."

"And you've never been busted?"

"Never. Now tell me I'm incompetent."

Levinsky shook his head. How was he supposed to get through to her? Being reasonable didn't work. Yelling at her didn't work. He sighed. "Mrs. Draper, it doesn't look good to jump over a table and beat the shit out of one of the top lawyers in the city."

But this only made Claudia smile. "It might not have looked good," she told Levinsky, "but it sure felt good. What was I supposed to do, sit there like a good girl and listen to my own lawyer say I wasn't competent to stand trial?"

Levinsky looked Claudia directly in the eyes. "Are you?"

Claudia pushed her hair back from her face. "How competent do you have to *be*, for chrissake?"

Levinsky thought about that one. "All right," he said finally. "Let's say, for the moment, that you're not *entirely* incompetent."

With a smug grin, Claudia nodded. "Yeah, let's say that."

"And," Levinsky went on hypothetically, "let's say the doctors are wrong."

Claudia grinned wider. "Let's say that, too."

Levinsky looked at Claudia quizzically. "So why," he asked, "is all this happening to you?"

For a second, Claudia's face went absolutely blank, as though someone had pulled a plug on her. But then she blinked, looked away, and a pained expression crossed her features.

Claudia's response intrigued Levinsky. As a lawyer, he knew that when a client didn't answer a question, you could be sure the client was hiding something. And the look of pain Levinsky had seen flash across Claudia's face indicated to him that whatever she was hiding hurt her so much she was willing to risk institutionalization rather than talk about it. But how much credence were you to put in a mere expression made by someone who might be crazy? *Was* Claudia trying to tell him something? Or was she merely demonstrating her craziness?

Levinsky decided to push a little bit. "Maybe," he said, "your mother and father think you need help."

Claudia's eyes flashed furiously. "They think I'm an embarrassment." And then she added, "Besides, Arthur isn't my real father. He's my stepfather."

Levinsky felt he was starting to get somewhere. He remembered Arthur King standing in the corridor outside the courtroom. What had he said? "I'm the girl's father and this is my wife." And then in the courtroom itself, Kirk had been yelling, "That's my daughter." Now, here was Claudia going out of her way to differentiate between a real father and a stepfather. Was there some significance in the fact that Claudia wanted Levinsky to know Kirk wasn't her real father while Kirk himself had obviously been wanting Levinsky to think he was?

It was late. Levinsky was exhausted and knew he had to decide quickly whether he was going to appear before Judge Box tomorrow and make a motion for commitment or for a sanity hearing. So what did he have to go on? Two psychiatrists saying his client was crazy. A client who insisted she wasn't but who refused to be interviewed by a third psychiatrist. The odds of Judge Box dismissing the findings of Arantes and Morrison were infinitely small without expert testimony from a third psychiatrist.

And then there was the matter of the client herself. If the woman wasn't actually insane, she certainly had a violent temper, which led her to *act* insane every time somebody . . . What? What kept triggering her violence? Levinsky suspected something was at the root of Claudia's reactions, but he couldn't for the life of him begin to figure out what it was. And if he couldn't get to that root, how was he to prove Claudia sane?

Levinsky thought about how Claudia had refused to answer his question as to why people wanted to put her away. Was she trying to tell him something? She who found it so easy to flash her body. Did she have a harder time flashing her mind?

For several seconds, Levinsky sat studying Claudia as though she were a textbook he couldn't quite grasp but knew he had to comprehend if he were to do well on a test. Was it possible for him to make a case before Judge Box for the woman's sanity? In order to do it, he would have to break through Claudia's sarcasm, her hostility, and her moods to find her motivations. Two psychiatrists hadn't been able to do this, why did he think a schlemiel could?

And yet something in Levinsky felt that he could. He had that tip-of-the-tongue sense about Claudia. And so he finally asked, "You want me to represent you at a competency hearing?"

If Claudia was at all grateful, she took pains to hide it. She eyed Levinsky suspiciously. "Are you any good?"

Levinsky shrugged. "You had good, now you got me."

"Oh," Claudia said, "I could do worse."

A smile started to grow on Levinsky's face. Although Claudia's words weren't exactly the greatest compliment in the history of mankind, they were thrilling to Levinsky's praise-starved ears. Still, he couldn't let her get false ideas about his ability to save her neck. "Don't be too sure," he said. "If we win the hearing, you get a trial. If you lose the trial, you could go to jail for twenty-five years."

Claudia gave Levinsky's necktie another disapproving glance, then looked up at his eyes. "Well, I'll take the risk. If I don't, I could wind up wearing this nightie until I collect social security."

"All right," Levinsky said, taking a legal pad from his briefcase. "Let's start at the beginning. MacMillan'll eat me alive, but give me some background details."

Claudia sat down beside Levinsky at the table. "Fine," she said. "Just talk to me and pretend I'm sane, okay?"

"Okay."

"And I'll do the same for you," she added generously.

"Thanks," Levinsky said, hoping against hope that perhaps they *were* both sane, but fearing that neither one of them truly was.

THREE

The next morning, Levinsky appeared before Judge Box and put forward a motion that Claudia be granted a competency hearing. The judge rolled his eyes at what he perceived as Levinsky's self-destructive stubbornness, but he granted the motion all the same. If Levinsky wanted to make a fool of himself in public, it was his business. He gave Levinsky four days to prepare his case.

Levinsky knew the judge thought he was wrong-headed, and he also knew that if he wasn't able to control Claudia's violence in the courtroom, he would probably never be given another client again by Judge Box. But he felt lighthearted all the same. On the subway into Manhattan his face hadn't looked half so haggard to him as it had the day before, and when he'd reached the escalator at Lexington Avenue, he had decided to take the steps instead.

There was a springiness to Levinsky's walk and a jauntiness to his shoulders as he moved through the corridor outside the courtroom. Levinsky didn't know why he was feeling so good, but his mind kept playing back to him the compliment Claudia had given him the night before. "I could do worse," she had said. She believed in him as a lawyer in a way she hadn't believed in the hotshot Clarence Middleton. And so what if she weren't the most levelheaded human being on the face of the planet? Thirsty men don't question who's pouring the water, they just drink. And Levinsky was drinking in Claudia's confidence that he could prove her sane.

Levinsky saw Kreiglitz's boss, Frank MacMillan, walking ahead of him in the corridor and ran to catch up. "Hey, MacMillan," he called out. "Frank!"

MacMillan turned around. He could tell there was something different about Levinsky. The man actually appeared to be in a good mood, for one thing. For another, Levinsky didn't seem quite as sloppy as usual. "Yeah, Aaron?" he asked. "What's up?"

"The Claudia Draper thing," Levinsky said proudly. "I've decided to go ahead with it."

Thinking that Levinsky meant he had seen the light at last and was going to go ahead with committing Claudia, MacMillan beamed and gave Levinsky a slap on the back. "Good! Good!"

Levinsky was puzzled by MacMillan's pleasure, then realized what the man was thinking and laughed. "No," he explained, "I'm gonna defend the girl at a competency hearing. The judge set it up for Monday."

MacMillan's face turned to stone and he quickly

withdrew his arm from Levinsky's back. So Levinsky hadn't turned over a new leaf after all; he was still the same jerk he'd always been. MacMillan shook his head. "Why would you want to do that? She'd be much better off in a hospital than she'd be in a prison." And then he added with significance, "Don't mess it up."

But Levinsky didn't even try to deal with MacMillan's criticism. He merely shrugged and said, "She wants to stand trial on the manslaughter charge and I think she's up to it."

MacMillan started walking away. "You do, huh?"

Levinsky followed, still good-natured. "Yeah, I do. So I'm going to need a few things. Police reports, court order to enter her apartment."

The corridor was crowded with people smoking cigarettes and drinking various beverages hidden in brown paper sacks. MacMillan pushed along past a group of what appeared to be motorcylists as Levinsky followed him.

"You're making a big mistake, Aaron. The girl is sick."

Levinsky shrugged as MacMillan turned into a men's room. "I got an aunt in Long Island more crazy than she is," Levinsky said, entering the bathroom on MacMillan's heels, "and nobody's locked her up."

MacMillan went over to one of the urinals. "It's a bad career move."

Staring at the graffiti-covered bathroom walls, Levinsky snorted. "You call this a career?"

What is it with this guy? MacMillan wondered.

Most men had ambitions to do something with their lives, make something of themselves, but all Levinsky ever seemed to do was try to make trouble. He didn't have the vaguest understanding of social hierarchies, of working your way up in the system. "Listen," MacMillan said patiently. "Arthur Kirk is very well connected. He doesn't want his daughter going through a long, lurid trial. We're doing her a favor."

But Levinsky didn't take the hint. "The accused wants her day in court," he said. "I still believe in that kind of stuff. Don't you?"

MacMillan glanced over at Levinsky. The guy was like some idealistic college student who thought anybody making a decent salary was corrupt, and anybody bucking the system was heroic. It was hard to believe sometimes that Levinsky was in his forties. But there he was, living in some crummy apartment in Forest Hills, going nowhere, tilting at windmills. "Don't get high and mighty on me," MacMillan said.

Levinsky smiled. "You know what, Francis? Maybe you don't think you have a good enough case, and you're trying to avoid a trial."

"I don't have a good enough case?" MacMillan asked indignantly. "The accused damn near cut off a john's head. What do you want to do, put her back on the streets and see who she kills next?"

MacMillan zipped up his pants and walked over to the sink, shaking his head at Levinsky's nerve. If ever there was a case MacMillan was sure to win, it was this one. Claudia Draper didn't just have two psychiatrists claiming she was nuts, she also had gone out of her way to prove she was nuts by her actions in front of the judge the other day.

But Levinsky wouldn't let up. He went over to the sink where MacMillan hovered. "Are you going to have your secretary pull those police reports?"

MacMillan shook his head. "She's got more important things to do."

But Levinsky didn't back off. Smiling confidently, he crossed his arms and said, "Then I'm going to paper you to death, Francis, and you're going to have to hire another secretary just to keep up with all the work."

MacMillan gave Levinsky a long, serious stare. "You'll be going up against me on this," he said.

Levinsky grinned with pleasure. "I'll try to make it interesting for you."

And then Levinsky walked briskly out of the bathroom, humming cheerfully as MacMillan, furious, watched him leave.

Over in the psychiatric ward of the New York County Prison Hospital, the patients were sitting in their gloomy lounge. They were supposed to be "practicing socialization skills in a nurturing, noncompetitive environment," according to the nurse who was supervising them, but what they were actually doing was hanging out. Some stared at an ancient, blurry-screened television in the corner of the room, while most wandered around dull-eyed, lost in their memories and delusions. Only the cardplayers in the middle of the room bothered to speak to each other at all, and most of their conversation consisted of paranoid complaints about cheating at seven-card stud.

Claudia walked about the lounge with a little note pad, writing down observations of her fellow patients. Every few minutes, the nurse told Claudia that she was not supposed to be doing this under orders from Dr. Morrison, but Claudia merely stuck her tongue out at the nurse and continued. She had been taking notes copiously since she had been admitted, and had no intention of stopping just because one of the hospital's many hundreds of rules forbade "private diaries."

This place, Claudia wrote in tiny script, *makes* One Flew over the Cuckoo's Nest *seem like* Little House on the Prairie. *People on the outside don't understand what it is to be nothing, to have nothing to do, nothing to think about. They think the horror of a loony bin is electric shock therapy or some midnight lobotomy. They don't know the horror is emptiness. We sit in this lounge day after day in our pajamas and robes, waiting to recover from some illness that makes us unfit for the real world. We are too sad, they tell us, or too happy, or too angry, or too mean. What they mean is we are too much. Old Agnes sitting on the couch has been here twenty years. She shot her husband after finding him in bed with her mother. She was "too emotional." So now she is "too withdrawn." Too withdrawn? The woman has to be reminded to go to the bathroom. I've heard when Agnes first came here she screamed and cried and swore the moment they let her out she was going to go blast her mother to smithereens. They say she had red hair once, and eyes that shone with her furious passions. She howled in the night at her double betrayal, ranted in her nightmares at her scumbag of a husband: "I loved you!" she yelled. "How could you!" Well, now she doesn't rant or howl or scream or cry anymore. They fixed that with their emptiness, their drugs, their cloth restraints. And me. Am I going to wind up Agnes, Part II? Last night I got a new lawyer. His name's Aaron Levinsky. I don't know what to think. Last week's lawyer was a pretentious WASP. This week's lawyer is a smart-ass Jew. Is there a difference between lawyers? Is there, actually, a difference between men?*

Claudia stopped writing, reread the last sentence in her pad, then slammed the pad shut and walked over to the cardplaying patients. She stood behind a timid woman named Suzanne who always lost, no matter what game was being played.

The woman dealing the cards gave Claudia an annoyed look and said, "How many, Suzanne?"

Suzanne stared at the cards in her hand with bewilderment. Her hands trembled. She seemed utterly incapable of making so minor a decision as how many cards she wanted to exchange, and looked about to cry.

Claudia looked at Suzanne's cards and whispered, "Stand pat."

"Stand pat?" Suzanne asked in a soft, frightened voice.

"Stand pat," Claudia said reassuringly. "You have a good hand."

Suzanne started to smile with gratitude when another patient—a large, heavy woman—banged her fist down on the table and said, "Hey! That's not fair."

"She just learned how to play," Claudia said, and nodded to Suzanne to go ahead.

But the stress and disapproval was too much for Suzanne. Her face melted with tears, and she flung her cards to the floor.

The nurse supervising the patients gave Claudia a superior look, as though to say, "You see the trouble you cause when you try to fill up the emptiness with something other than drugs and sleep?" But Claudia was determined not to give in to the nothingness of being a zombie and she wanted to make Suzanne stop being a zombie, too. So she dove under the table and tried to rescue Suzanne's cards. "No, Suzanne!" she said excitedly. "You're going to *win*! You've got three kings and two jacks. A full house!"

Claudia waved the cards happily in Suzanne's sad face and slowly Suzanne's eyes began to shine. Claudia felt a wave of triumph, but then she heard a stern voice call out to her.

Looking out from under the table, Claudia saw Dr. Morrison stare at her with obvious loathing. For a moment, Claudia considered staying under the table, forcing the doctor to come down to his hands and knees to drag her out. Then when Morrison was down on the floor like a baby, she and the other patients could grab him and tie him up in restraints.

Claudia glanced at the patients at the card table. All of them were eying Morrison like frightened rabbits. The gleam in Suzanne was gone now. Her eyes blinked timidly at the doctor. And the other patients bowed their heads deferentially as though Morrison was the pope or something.

Claudia sighed. Her fellow patients were obviously not up for acting out a scene from *Mutiny on the Bounty*. And alone, she was powerless against Morrison's army of orderlies, nurses, and hypodermic needles containing sleep-inducing sedatives.

"Would you like to come in now, Claudia?" Morrison asked, gesturing toward his office along the corridor.

"*Would* I like to?" Claudia replied sarcastically.

Morrison grimaced as though he were being forced to deal with an unruly two-year-old. "Let me put it this way," he said. "Come into my office, Claudia."

For a time, Claudia remained under her table as Morrison strutted off to his office, then she got to her feet, gave her fellow patients a salute, and goose-stepped after Morrison into an immaculate white room where he waited for her behind his large, tidy desk.

The room itself got on Claudia's nerves. Its cleanliness annoyed her—she could picture Morrison wiping off his patients' fingerprints after they left—but mainly what she hated were the cartoons Morrison had neatly clipped from the *New Yorker* and hung on the wall over his desk. They were polite, witty cartoons, all intellect and no feeling.

The sort of not-too-funny cartoons smart people like to chuckle over to show how smart they are. Every time Claudia was forced to look at them, she felt like ripping them down and force-feeding them to Morrison. It would be fun to make him eat his own pretentious words.

Claudia also couldn't stomach the photograph Morrison kept of his family on his desk. Sometimes when she came in the office, she turned it facedown, but today she just glared at it. There they were: Ozzie and Harriet Nelson and their sickeningly sweet kids. The picture was so wholesome in its view of the American family that it even included a dog. Claudia stared at Mrs. Morrison—her hair beauty-parlor perfect, her clothes so discreet and tasteful. Poor woman, Claudia thought, she doesn't even get paid to sleep with a bimbo like Morrison.

Morrison took out a file on Claudia from his desk. Claudia, in turn, flipped open her notebook and wrote *Thursday afternoon: Meeting with Dr. Frankenstein.*

"I see you're still taking notes," Morrison said.

Claudia grinned. "I have a feeling I'll need them."

Morrison folded his hands across his desk. "Need them for what?"

"Some guys are trying to put me away," Claudia explained.

Gazing up at the ceiling of his office, Morrison said, "When you say 'some guys,' who do you mean exactly?"

Claudia wrote: *The shrink who told the court I'm*

crazy is asking me who I think is trying to get me committed.

Morrison watched Claudia scribble for a moment, then went on. "Do you mean men in general, or do you have some specific men in mind?"

Claudia glanced up from her note pad. "What do you want?" she asked.

"I want to talk to you," Morrison said patiently.

"Well, I don't want to talk to *you,*" Claudia said. "The last time I talked to you, you and Pancho Villa asked me a bunch of stupid questions and called me incompetent."

Morrison sighed. "It would be better if you could trust me."

Claudia stared at Morrison incredulously. "Why? 'Cause you have a degree? What do you guys do, work on commission?"

For a time, Morrison didn't reply. Claudia could hear his foot tapping under his desk. That's right, Herbie, Claudia thought, get rid of all that tension through displacement. You'd like to kick my head in but you'll kick the floor instead like a good boy.

At last Morrison rose and walked over to a coffeemaker in the corner of his office. "Would you like a cup?" he asked Claudia.

"Not unles there's Thorazine in it," Claudia asked.

Morrison smiled indulgently. "Sorry. Only milk and sugar."

"Pass," Claudia said. And in her notebook she wrote: *Wants to gain my trust by giving me coffee. I guess when he works with kids he tries to gain their trust with milk, and with old people it must be prune juice.*

Where did this guy go to medical school anyhow? Probably some place advertised in a matchbook: "You too can enter the glamorous and exciting field of psychiatry in just thirty days or your money back."

Morrison finished pouring his coffee and returned to his desk. For a while he sipped at his coffee and watched Claudia write, then he said, "I heard you had quite a violent episode in court yesterday. I heard you couldn't control your anger."

"No I couldn't!" Claudia shouted. "How do you expect me to act? Dead? Where does it say I have to be nice to get a fair trial?"

"You're getting angry again," Morrison said in a gentle singsong voice.

Claudia leaned over toward him. "Yeah, I got a lot to be angry about. I live in New York City, for Christ's sake. I got three locks on my door. Ever try getting crosstown during rush hour?"

"We all have these feelings, Claudia, but we learn to control them."

Claudia leaned across Morrison's desk and looked him in the eyes. "Don't you ever lose control, Herbie?" she asked. "Don't you ever let yourself go?"

Morrison leaned back in his chair, putting some distance between himself and Claudia. Soundlessly, he counted to ten, and then he said out loud, "You're a very frightened girl, and under stress you can become dangerous to others and yourself. That's what I plan to say in court. You need treatment in order to be able to control yourself."

Suddenly, Claudia stood up and walked around

Morrison's desk. "Oh, I'm in control, Herbie," she said, standing right over him, " 'cause I'd like to wring your fucking neck right now, but I'm not going to."

Morrison's foot tapped violently beneath his desk, but he managed to stay calm. "Good," he said in a voice that was only slightly strained. "That's a step in the right direction. I'd like to help you put your life back in order."

Claudia laughed. "But, Herbie, there *is* no order in life. Maybe you need order. Maybe that's why you're here, behind bars, makes you feel safe, doesn't it?"

For a moment, Morrison looked as though he was about to slap Claudia, but then he glanced at the photo of his family and quietly said, "Do you think this is productive?"

By way of response, Claudia gave Morrison's chair a kick and then walked away from him. She intended to bolt out of his office, but when she reached the door, instead of leaving, she spun around and said, "You ever ride the subway, Herbie?"

Morrison gave her a puzzled stare.

"Ever mix in with the people?" she went on. "You don't like people, do you? I know you, Herbie. You see, I know you better than you know me. Because I've seen you with your pants down. I know how your mind works. You drop your pants and talk about your fears. You have to sit in the aisle, don't you, Herbie? No subway for you. Too many strangers, too much disorder, too many surprises. This place suits you fine, doesn't it, Herbie? It's home."

Morrizon gazed at Claudia but said nothing. He didn't have to say anything. He had already decided that as soon as his session with her was finished, he was going to have her tied to her bed and heavily sedated. For her own good, of course.

That afternoon, as Claudia lay in a drugged stupor, Levinsky managed to get a permit to enter her apartment. It hadn't been easy to talk MacMillan into coming up with the permit, but MacMillan's secretary had come to his aid. The woman chain-smoked Kools and when Levinsky brought her a carton she became extremely sympathetic to his plight and leaned on her boss.

So Levinsky took off for the ritzy upper-east-side apartment building where Claudia lived. He ate a peanut-butter-and-jelly sandwich on the bus ride over and looked out the window as the bus moved from the sleazy, dilapidated neighborhood where Levinsky worked to Claudia's sleek, upper-class neighborhood. Women whose faces had been lifted so often their eyes turned up at the corners walked haughtily along the litter-free sidewalks with pastel-dyed Pekingese dogs wearing jeweled collars. Ordinarily, seeing women like that made Levinsky's ulcer flair up, but today he merely grinned at them.

The bus swept past the kind of peculiar boutiques that reminded Levinsky more of movie sets than stores. He knew Claudia must shop in those boutiques. He pictured her coming out of a florist's, her brown hair blowing, her arms full of exotic flowers, but then he caught himself and thought that just because the woman had flashed her body at him didn't give him the right to start up some teenage fantasy. Don't be an idiot, he told himself, and go and get a crush on a hooker indicted for manslaughter. He tried to imagine his wife coming out of the florist's instead, but that *did* make Levinsky's ulcer flair up.

Levinsky leaned back in the seat of the bus and tried to remember why he had married his wife in the first place. Had he actually proposed to her? Had she proposed to him? To the best of his recollection, neither of them had ever been stupid enough to want to marry the other. Even in the early days of their relationship, they had been more like Ralph and Alice Kramden than the Duke and Duchess of Windsor. Just two dumb kids from Queens. They had met at a Vietnam peace rally at Columbia. A thunderstorm broke out on campus that day and everyone except her ran for cover. He stood under a balcony at the student union and watched her as she'd crashed through huge puddles in these funny-looking red Keds sneakers. A strange-looking girl, purple in the face as she shouted, "Hell no! We won't go!" Even when lightning had filled the sky, she kept marching. There was something about her hair that captured Levinsky's heart for a moment. She had these pigtails tied in a pink yarn that kept slapping at her face as she walked, lonely and wet, through the rain.

Those pigtails did me in, Levinsky thought sadly as he recalled running over to her—more full of pity than lust—and saying, "Hey girly! The war's not gonna end any faster just because you get yourself electrocuted." She looked at him with a fury that he would come to know well over the years and yelled, "I don't need some male chauvinist pig telling me what to do."

An inauspicious beginning . . . but somehow they'd wound up going for coffee, where they'd learned they were both scholarship students, Jews, social rejects, and virgins. Her name was Nancy Shwartz. "You wouldn't even have to meet me to know I'm a dog, would you?" she asked. "With a name like Nancy Shwartz, you just know you're dealing with someone who's got acne, bowed legs, and frizzy hair. "I like your hair," Levinsky had said. "Yeah? What about my acne?" she sneered.

Well, he didn't really mind the acne, or the bowed legs either. He told her she wasn't really so ugly, and she told him him he wasn't really such a chauvinist pig, and before too long neither of them was a virgin anymore. . . .

Suddenly, Levinsky realized he'd overshot his bus stop. He pulled the cord, got off at the next intersection, and ran over to a swank doorman building in the sixties.

The lobby alone was impressive with its mahogany trim, sculpted ceiling, and its indescribable scent of money. Levinsky breathed deeply as the doorman escorted him to the elevator, which brought him up to Claudia's apartment, where the building's superintendent was waiting to let him in.

"You with the police?" the super asked.

"Sort of," Levinsky said.

"This is the first murder we ever had in here," the super went on. "It's a good building. A safe building."

"I'm sure it is," Levinsky assured him, and then went in alone.

The living room shocked Levinsky's senses, not because it had been the scene of a murder and still bore signs of the struggle that had taken place between Claudia and the man she was charged with killing, but because even with the smashed lamps, the overturned furniture, and the dried blood stains, it was still the most sensuous room Levinsky had ever seen.

The decor was subtly Oriental. There were pieces of jade, shoji screens, and soft pillows covered in exotic material. On the floor was a dense fur rug. Levinsky waded through it with the peculiar feeling that he was walking over something upon which Claudia had no doubt made love.

His eyes were dazzled everywhere he turned. There were mirrors, candles, lushly stuffed furniture, and even a complete bar. The perfect love nest for a weary businessman far away from home. Everything was designed to be comfortable, relaxing, and especially erotic. And yet there was nothing too personal—no photographs, no mementos, no traces of who Claudia was other than that she was a woman who knew how to please a man.

Levinsky wandered into the bedroom. If he'd thought the living room was sexy, he hadn't *known* sexy. The bed was surrounded with black gauze curtains, which gave it the look of a mysterious cocoon or womb. The bed, which was king size, was stripped, but Levinsky could imagine it with satin sheets. He started to picture Claudia lying in the bed, naked, but pulled back from the thought, for no sooner did he start to imagine her breasts, her hips, than he also started to imagine some customer of hers touching those breasts, those hips.

In the bedroom, the only personal touch was a ceramic hand that held rings. Levinsky went over to it, stared at the glittering rings as though they could help him understand Claudia better, but they offered no clues.

Levinsky turned toward Claudia's closet. He had an athletic bag with him because he wanted to pick up some clothes for Claudia that would be more appropriate for the witness stand than her pajama and robe set from the institution. But as he headed toward the closet, he happened to pass by the entrance to the bathroom—the room in which Claudia had, according to police reports, slashed the neck of one of her customers.

The mirror in the all-white room was shattered, and the floor was stained a reddish brown with blood. Levinsky stared at the floor, feeling a little queasy from all the blood, when suddenly the telephone rang and made him jump.

Immediately after the phone's first ring, Claudia's voice came on an answering machine. "This is 555-1246," she whispered in a husky voice, "but I'm more than a number. Talk to me."

Levinsky walked back into the bedroom and searched for the telephone as a man's voice came on the machine: "This is Mr. K. Back at the Tower Hotel, room 671. I have a tip on some telecommunications stock you might find interesting. Come on over and we'll talk. Have a little fun. Call me."

Wandering into the living room, Levinsky continued looking for the telephone and answering machine. He went over to a window and pulled back the curtain, thinking maybe the phone was sitting behind it on the ledge. But what he found startled him. Instead of the curtain leading to a window, it led to a small alcove—a kind of secret apartment.

Levinsky walked into the alcove with a smile of discovery on his face. He felt like Sherlock Holmes as he stared around Claudia's "real" apartment, a room full of books, paintings, cozy sweaters, blue jeans, and even a goldfish bowl.

Eyeing an old desk in a corner that was covered with some of Levinsky's favorite novels—*Middlemarch, Tender Is the Night, All the King's Men,* and *Beyond the Bedroom Wall*—Levinsky began to laugh. So the happy hooker was a closet intellectual who spent her free time hiding out from her sexuality in a world of ideas.

The telephone and answering machine were next to the books. Levinsky flipped the answering machine cassette to the beginning of the tape and begun playing back Claudia's messages while he explored her hidden alcove.

The first message was pretty straightforward: "Mrs. Draper, your VCR is ready. Gimme a call when you want it delivered."

Levinsky walked over to Claudia's goldfish bowl and tapped some fish food into it. The goldfish lapped up their food as though they were close to starvation.

The second message started: "Hi, Claudia. I'm a friend of . . . er, Lee . . . do you remember Lee? Big guy, dark hair, glasses. He's with Allied? Anyway, he suggested I give you a ring . . . Damn, I hate talking to these things. I feel like an idiot . . . My name is Allen. I'm at 555-9970 . . . Could you call me? I'd really like that. Lee says . . . I'd *really* like it; 555-9970."

Levinsky left the alcove and went to Claudia's closet as the message continued to play. He opened the door and was amazed by all the glittery, feathered, and shining dresses Claudia owned, and wondered if she had anything that would be suitable for the courtroom.

The third message came over the answering machine. "Mrs. Draper, it's the super. You can't use your intercom till tomorrow. I have to get a part for it."

Levinsky searched through Claudia's dresses until he came upon one that at least didn't seem to glow in the dark. It had a fairly high neckline, too. He removed it from its hanger, rolled it up awkwardly, and shoved it into his athletic bag as he listened to a message from Claudia's dry cleaner. Then he went over to Claudia's dresser, looking for a slip to bring with the dress, but the top drawer was filled only with underpants of every conceivable—and inconceivable—style. There were crotchless underpants, laced underpants, satin underpants.

Hesitantly, Levinsky touched the panties, thinking he should probably bring Claudia a pair of those as well. He waded through the black ruffled ones with embarrassment and some wonder, until he came across a pair that he could see handing over to Claudia without his face turning red.

Something was at the bottom of the underwear drawer. Levinsky reached and came up with some photographs of Claudia. They were erotic pictures, but more sensuous that lewd. One in particular captured Levinsky's attention—a portrait of Claudia taken from the back, looking out a window. In it, the breeze from the window blew a curtain against the tilt of her breast and the curve of her thigh. Pieces of sunlight touched her cheek, her breast, and the point of her hip.

Holding the picture close to his face, Levinsky stared at it as though he was a man who had just been given sight. He was astonished by the serenity in Claudia's pose, and by the beauty in her features. Something deep in him wished that he could bring what he saw in the photograph into the woman he had met the night before. He wanted to take away her fury and bring her grace.

Another message came on the machine: "This is Allen again. Sorry to bother you, but I had a tough day. I need to relax. I'll be at the Walnut Room at seven-thirty. Ask for Mr. Green. Don't disappoint me, Claudia."

Levinsky turned toward the answering machine, then back to the photograph of Claudia. It seemed impossible that the woman in the picture could let herself be touched for any reason other than love. But then so many things about Claudia didn't add up. She almost seemed to be two people: the Claudia of the hidden alcove and the Claudia of the black crotchless panties. Where was the point of intersection between the two lines of Claudia's life? Levinsky needed to find it if he was to help remove her from the institution. But so far, she hadn't shown any willingness to reveal herself to him.

For a moment, Levinsky started to put the photograph back into Claudia's drawer, but then he stopped, stared at it again, and quickly stashed it into his briefcase. For reference, he told himself, but his heart was telling him something else.

FOUR

Later that afternoon, Levinsky tried to reach Claudia on the phone to let her know he would be coming by the hospital that evening for another meeting, but the attendant who answered the telephone said that under orders from Dr. Morrison, Claudia could neither receive visitors nor speak to outsiders until further notice was given. The attendant wouldn't say why.

Levinsky hung up the phone, furious. Just how was he supposed to create a case and defend Claudia if he couldn't even talk to her? He suspected that Morrison was trying to thwart his efforts, but how to prove this? He placed several calls to administrators at the hospital and explained how imperative it was that a lawyer be allowed to meet with a client before appearing in court. At last, no doubt weary of Levinsky's persistent phoning, the head of the hospital called him and agreed that Levinsky could visit with Claudia the next day, Friday, for an hour.

On Friday, Levinsky once again found himself trying to make his way through the maze of colored lines on the hospital floor. With his briefcase and the athletic bag, he nervously plodded along the ancient hallways. What if Claudia remained uncommunicative about her life? What if he had to show up in court without any answers? The district attorney would be sure to discuss Claudia's seemingly gratuitous decision to become a prostitute. How was Levinsky to prove that a perfectly sane woman could leave her husband and set herself up as a call girl? How was he to refute the findings of the psychiatrists? Even if Claudia behaved perfectly in the courtroom—which seemed like an unrealistic hope to Levinsky—was there any real chance of proving her actions sane?

At last, Levinsky made it to the cage outside the psychiatric ward. The attendant grimaced at him, but let him through the barred door nonetheless. Together they walked along the corridor until they reached the lounge.

Claudia sat on a plastic chair at the nurses' station. She was talking to an older woman who was seated behind a desk. The woman was in her fifties, and from her white coat and professional conversation, Levinsky could tell she was a psychiatrist.

As Levinsky approached Claudia, he could hear her saying, "Of course, doctor, I see your point." And then she glanced up and grinned at Levinsky.

"Hey Levinsky!" Claudia called out. "Are you ready for this? A doctor who makes sense."

Levinsky went over to the two women and exchanged smiles with the doctor.

"She and I have been talking for hours," Claudia went on.

"Really?" Levinsky asked excitedly. Maybe here was the break he'd been looking for. If Claudia could get this doctor to testify on her behalf Monday, the case might not be so difficult after all.

Levinsky hurriedly pulled up a chair. "May I join in?" he asked the doctor.

"Please," the doctor said pleasantly. "We're talking about the nature of paranoia, a subject of occasional interest around here."

Claudia nodded. "To put it in a nutshell, Levinsky, the lady says I don't need a hospital, I need a nice walk down Fifth Avenue."

Levinsky beamed at the doctor. Pay dirt! "So you don't agree with Morrison's diagnosis?"

The doctor, bless her heart, shook her head. "I won't deny that Claudia can benefit from therapy, but it could be conducted on an outpatient basis. Twice a week to start with, I should think, leading to a group therapy situation once a week."

"This is terrific," Claudia said, looking at Levinsky with pleasure. "This is just what we needed."

Levinsky leaned over to the doctor. "Would you be prepared to testify at Claudia's hearing Monday?"

Suddenly, the doctor became very quiet and began to fidgit. "Monday? And what's today? Friday? Oh, my . . . Friday. Oh my . . . a weekend."

At first Levinsky didn't understand. What skin

was it off the doctor's back to agree on a Friday to testify on a Monday? What was making her so upset?

The doctor played with the buttons on her white coat. "Monday, you say. Well, I'll have to check my calendar. Monday is the day . . . I . . ." And then her voice trailed off as she stood up.

Levinsky's jaw dropped as he saw the doctor walk away from the desk where she had been sitting. Beneath her white coat was a hospital gown!

The woman gave Levinsky a nervous smile. "One of my secretaries will be in touch with you," she said, and then she scurried away to another corner of the lounge.

Claudia laughed for some time as Levinsky sat with his face buried morosely in his hands. Then she said, "Oh cheer up. You don't want people thinking you're nuts."

At last Levinsky took his hands away from his face. He eyed Claudia. "*Very* cute," he said.

Still smiling, Claudia shrugged. "She really is a doctor. A chiropractor, sort of."

Levinsky looked over at the woman. She had joined a group of the other patients staring at the fuzzy TV screen. How could he have fallen for Claudia's neat little trick? Now that he looked at "the doctor," he saw she had an obviously crazed appearance. What had prevented him from noticing her insanity earlier? And what about Claudia? Could the whole world tell she was nuts except for Levinsky?

Claudia chuckled again and Levinsky turned to her. Was the gleam in her eyes mad?

Levinsky sighed. Well, mad or not, she was his client. He was stuck with her violent episodes, her smart-aleck talk, her practical jokes. So he opened up his briefcase and tossed her a sandwich he'd gotten at a deli. "Here," he said. "Hope you like a lot of mustard."

"For me?" Claudia asked.

Levinsky nodded.

Claudia unwrapped her sandwich with glee. "Food! Honest-to-God food!"

"Pastrami."

"Pastrami!" And then with a wink: "You're okay, Levinsky."

Levinsky opened his mouth to say something, then stopped and glanced over at the woman who had been posing as a psychiatrist. "She looked so normal."

Claudia ate away at her sandwich as though she hadn't seen food in a year. In between ravenous bites, she said, "She poisoned her husband."

Levinsky shuddered, then turned back to his briefcase. He removed a thick law text from it and handed it over to Claudia. "We're on for Monday, ten o'clock." And as he tapped the book: "I've marked some places here. Study them."

For a while, Claudia seemed more fascinated by her pastrami sandwich than by her law case, but eventually she finished eating and glanced at Levinsky. "You seem nervous."

"I wish I had more time," Levinsky said honestly.

"Relax," Claudia said. "You'll do fine."

Not if you don't start talking to me, Levinsky thought. But he didn't want to push her immediately, so he reached for his athletic bag and said, "Here, I've brought you some clothes to wear to the hearing."

"Claudia smiled widely. "You bought me clothes?"

"I *brought* you clothes," Levinsky said.

For a moment Claudia stared at Levinsky as he opened up the bag, and then she said, "From where?"

Levinsky could hear a change in her tone. He looked up at her, saw her eyes turning dark with anger. "From your apartment," he said innocently.

Claudia exploded with fury. "Who said you could go into my apartment? What did you take?"

"Just clothes," Levinsky said quietly. "A dress, shoes, a couple of things." What was the big deal? He'd thought she'd be pleased. "I want you to wear your own clothes in court," he explained.

But Claudia's face only became angrier. "Why didn't you ask me?" she demanded.

"Because there's no time. I'm *trying* to help you," he said removing the rolled-up clothing from the bag.

Claudia eyed her clothing, then gave Levinsky a sharp glance. Now she spoke to him through clenched teeth. "What gives you the right to invade me?"

"Invade you?" Levinsky asked incredulously. "I don't want you to look like a nut in court."

Claudia leaned over close to him. "When's the

last time you went through your wife's dresser?" she screamed. "When's the last time you scouted around her panty drawer?"

Levinsky could feel his face starting to burn with shame, but he said, "Calm down, for Christ's sake. It's no big deal."

But to Claudia, it obviously was a big deal. She jumped to her feet, hellfire burning in her eyes, and shouted: "When's the last time somebody went through your goddamn things without permission? It is a big deal. I decide who sees my underwear, wears my underwear, brings my underwear!"

The other patients in the room began to giggle and the attendant started to walk over. But Levinsky waved him away as he stood up and said, "I'm sorry . . . I'm sorry."

His words didn't appease Claudia, though. The fury in her eyes grew more and more intense until it turned into a steely, faraway stare.

I call the shots. I set the prices. I decide the hours. I tell them to come over. I tell them to get lost. Nobody tells me anything. They can touch me, suck me, lick me, kiss me, cuddle me, and screw me, but they can't tell me what to do. . . . That night the rain was falling. I wanted "Allen Green" to get the hell out. His hour was over, but he wouldn't get the message. I turned on a light, got out of bed, and went to my closet for a robe. When I came back, he was standing at my dresser, going through my underwear drawer. I decided to ignore him. I flopped down on the bed and reached over for my phone book. "I'd like to see you in this," he said, lifting up a pair of black lace panties. "Next week, my sweet," I explained.

But he pouted. "I don't want to go home tonight." I tried to be nice. I'd given him a bottle of wine; I'd given him my body; now I would give him a chance to make a graceful exit. "We had a good time tonight, baby," I said, "but now you have to go." He didn't listen. He walked into the bathroom. I started to dial my next trick on the phone as he turned on the water in the tub. "Hey," he called out, "let's take a nice, sexy bubble bath together." I kept trying to be patient: "I can't, sweetheart. You were so great you made me lose track of time. Now I have another appointment. I'm sorry." But he got pissed the way they sometimes did when it occurred to them they weren't the only men on the planet with a wallet and a penis. He yelled, "What're you gonna do now? Fuck somebody else?" I ignored him and talked to my next trick on the phone, told him I was sorry but was running a little late. The trick said he'd be waiting for me dressed up in his World War II uniform as usual. He was a guy who liked to pretend he was in foxholes when he got laid. I said that sounded wonderful and told him I'd be by in about half an hour. Then it was back to Allen, who was saying, "Where's your bubble bath? Ya got any bath salts, that kind of stuff?" I got off the bed and went over to the bathroom. On my way I glanced down at the ceramic hand where I kept my rings to make sure Allen had paid me. Sure enough, there were hundred-dollar bills wedged between each of the fingers. So now the only thing to do was force him out. I stood in the doorway and looked at him. "Allen," I said firmly, "be a good boy." He looked up at me with his yellow teeth showing. "Don't give me that whore talk," he said. I sighed. "It was a lot of fun, Allen, but time's up. That's enough." But he started walking toward me. Angry. A thwarted baby. "I say when it's enough," he told me, and then he started trying to take my robe off and get me in the bathtub with him. "I like to bathe girls," he whispered. My teeth started to chatter. I was feeling caught, over my head. "I'm not a girl anymore," I said, but I was scared. I was feeling like a girl again, and I hated that feeling, didn't want that terrible feeling back. I pushed him away, but he pulled me toward him. He thought it was a game. He grabbed me at my breasts, saying, "Well, you're not a boy." I shoved at him. He stumbled against the sink, banged his elbow on the corner. "Bitch!" My teeth were still chattering, but I glared at him and said, "I don't do baths!" He didn't understand how serious I was. He whined. "You sound like my wife . . . I don't do this, I don't do that.' " And then he tried to strike me. My heart was banging. I was terrified but knew better than to show him. "Stop it, Allen. I'm not your wife—calm down." He didn't calm down, though. He was losing control, hitting me harder. I tried to hold his fists away from me, but they crashed down against my shoulders, my breasts. He was stronger than I was, screaming, "You goddamn cunts are all alike." I ran from the room, tried to make it to my telephone, but suddenly he was right over me, ripping the cord out from the wall. I raced to the living room screaming, almost made it to the front door, but he grabbed me before I could get out. I raked my fingernails down his face, thinking maybe that would stop him. Nothing was going to stop him. His fist smashed into my cheekbone. His eyes were huge and crazy and I was gasping. I kneed him in the groin and as he bent over I grabbed a chromium decanter and begin swinging it. I heard it, didn't see it, but heard it crush into his face. I saw the blood then, his face turning red and wet. I could have stopped. I should have stopped. I should have stopped. But I . . . I kept smashing him with the decanter, screaming out each time it hit into his face. The blood flying out at me. He kept reaching for me, flying out at me. He kept reaching for me, finally got the decanter from my hands. I couldn't think anymore, just ran, and then I was in the bathroom again trying to slam the door, but he was after me, his bloody fingers coming at me. He threw the decanter at my head. I ducked and heard it shatter against the mirror. His bloody hands on my neck, squeezing me tighter and tighter. I couldn't stop choking, slid to the floor. My head banging on the floor over and over. Everything turning red and brown on me. And then I saw the glass from the mirror and reached for it even though I was so tired I couldn't breathe. I curled my fingers around the glass as hard as I could and then lifted my hand into his neck. . . .

Levinsky reached his hand out to Claudia. He could see in her eyes she was somewhere far away from him. He wanted to ask her where she was, wanted to reach her hiding place. But when his fingers touched her, she started to scream and wouldn't stop, even when the attendant came and took her away.

Sweating, Levinsky slumped down into a chair in the lounge. All the patients were staring at him, but he didn't care. He kept seeing Claudia's eyes, unblinking, terrified. He kept hearing her scream.

Levinsky looked at the pile of clothes he had

brought from her apartment. How could she have gotten so upset about his opening her dresser drawers? What was it she was keeping so deep inside her the only way it could come out was with a howl?

Leaving the clothes, Levinsky stood up and walked back down the corridor, his shoulders more slumped than they had been the other day when Seymour Cohen's limousine had left him standing in humiliation on the street corner. He walked slowly to the door, where another attendant let him out, and then he followed the maze of red lines through the hospital and back out onto the streets again.

The sun was setting. What was there to do now but get a drink and try not to think about Monday morning?

FIVE

Harry the Bailiff, a gentle-looking middle-aged man, stood at the grimy courtroom window adjusting the blinds. It was Monday morning, and the sky was gray from a rainstorm that was just ending as the court came into session.

Levinsky sat with his chin in his hand at the defense table. He watched Harry for a moment, stared at the bleak sky, then began to remove legal pads and files from his briefcase. He felt so low it was hard for him to believe that just a few days before he had stood triumphantly in this courtroom and asked Judge Box for a sanity hearing. Who was that man who had thought he had a chance to play the hero? Surely not Levinsky the Schlemiel.

All around Levinsky, people were filing into the courtroom with umbrellas and raincoats. The court reporter walked past him and went to her seat to check her equipment. Levinsky glanced her way and saw Dr. Morrison walk haughtily through the side entrance and take his seat. Then Claudia's mother and stepfather entered. They looked at Levinsky—Arthur Kirk with a cold stare, and Rose Kirk with her usual sad-eyed gaze—and then went to sit on the opposite side of the courtroom from the doctor.

Frank MacMillan came in next. He nodded curtly to Levinsky, then hurried over to the Kirks. Levinsky saw him speaking reassuringly to them. And why not? If Claudia was anything like she had been last Friday, the hearing would only take a minute or two, and then the Kirks could have their daughter safely tucked away in an institution where they believed she belonged and where, Levinsky had to begin to consider, maybe she *did* belong.

There was a murmur in the court and Levinsky turned around to see Claudia emerging from the prisoners' entrance with a police matron at her side. Only she wasn't the Claudia Levinsky was used to seeing. She was a transformed Claudia with makeup on, hair brushed attractively, and, wonder of wonders, dressed in the clothes Levinsky had brought her from her apartment on Friday.

Levinsky stood up with amazement. He couldn't believe his eyes. even her posture was different. She walked confidently, carrying the law book he had given her along with her little note pad. And she smiled graciously at him as she approached.

"You look wonderful," Levinsky said.

Claudia grinned and spun around for him. "You know what I use this dress for? For the ones who want to sit on Mommy's lap." And then she sat down and began to doodle on her note pad as Levinsky continued to eye her with disbelief.

Could it possibly be that Claudia was going to make it through the hearing without any kind of outbreak? And if she did, was it possible that maybe Levinsky could somehow pull off a miracle and get Judge Box to give her a chance to stand trial? Levinsky could feel some hope returning to his bones as he sat down beside Claudia. But then the door to the judge's chamber opened, and instead of Judge Box, out walked Judge Stanley Murdoch, the oldest and most conservative Judge Levinsky knew. Behind his back, lawyers referred to him as "Hang 'em High Stanley."

Levinsky tumbled into his seat, stunned by his own rotten luck. Here Claudia had gone and gotten herself together, only for Murdoch to ruin the day.

Harry the Bailiff was speaking: "All rise, please. His Honor, Stanley Murdoch, the Justice of the Court."

Everyone in the courtroom rose and Judge Murdoch took his seat at the bench. Then the judge signaled them to be seated and began. "This hearing has been set to controvert the findings of psychiatric examinations," he said evenly. "In the matter of the People of the State of New York *versus* Claudia Faith Draper. Is the defendant ready, Mr.—"

"Levinsky, your honor," the court recorder quickly interjected.

Great, Levinsky thought. The old man doesn't

even know my name. Then he stood up and said, "Your honor, let the record show that counsel for the defense has recommended independent psychiatric examination and testimony, and client has rejected that recommendation."

Judge Murdoch peered from Claudia to Levinsky over his bifocals with some curiosity and then said, "So noted."

Levinsky swallowed. "The defendant is ready your honor."

MacMillan stood up. "The People are ready, your honor."

The judge nodded and said, "Proceed, Mr. MacMillan."

Claudia leaned over to Levinsky. "Covering your ass?" she asked politely.

Levinsky grinned. "You bet."

And then the hearing began. Frank MacMillan walked assuredly up to the bench. "Your honor, the defendant has been indicted in the county of New York for a felony, namely, manslaughter in the first degree." He handed the judge a pile of reports. "As you can see from the papers before you, the two examining psychiatrists found the defendant did not have the capacity to stand trial. The defendant filed a motion for a hearing to challenge. This procedure is that hearing. Your honor, only one of the examining psychiatrists is present to testify, but since their findings were the same, I'd like to have a stipulation for the absent witness."

Levinsky sprang to his feet. "Objection, your honor."

"Overruled," the judge said without losing a beat.

"MacMillan's lips twitched with a smile. "Your honor, I'd like to call Dr. Herbert Morrison."

As Dr. Morrison walked quickly up to the witness stand to be sworn in, Claudia turned around and looked at her mother. Rose Kirk mouthed the words, "Hello, darling," and Arthur Kirk waved. But Claudia just stared and then spun back toward Morrison.

Harry the Bailiff was speaking. "Do you solemnly swear that the testimony you shall give in this special proceeding shall be the truth, the whole truth, and nothing but the truth?"

Morrison solemnly swore that it would indeed be that, and MacMillan stepped up to him. "Dr. Morrison," MacMillan began, "would you please tell the court your present position and place of employment, and something about your past experience in your profession."

"I have been a licensed psychiatrist for thirty years," Morrison said proudly. "I am currently the ward unit chief of New York County Prison Hospital."

Claudia laughed. "Couldn't make it on Park Avenue," she muttered to Levinsky.

"Shh," Levinsky whispered back.

"Or even Columbus," Claudia went on.

MacMillan gave Claudia a stare and turned to the judge. "Your honor . . ."

Levinsky tugged on the sleeve of Claudia's dress. "Quiet!" he said. But it was too late. The judge was looking at him.

"Mrs. Draper," the judge said, "please keep quiet." And then he glanced back to MacMillan. "Continue."

Levinsky drummed a pencil against his legal pads. He knew as far as Judge Murdoch was concerned, Claudia had already pushed the limits of the court's understanding to their utmost. Oh please Claudia, he thought, please keep your damn smart remarks to yourself.

MacMillan went on. "Dr. Morrison, have you examined the defendant, Claudia Draper?"

"Yes, I have," Morrison said.

"What did the examination consist of?"

Morrison sat up stiffly in his chair and announced, "The examination consisted of questions and answers, in the usual flow of a psychiatric interview, to ascertain the patient's mental condition."

"And how would you define the mental condition of the defendant?"

With a rapid glance at Claudia, Morrison said, "Initially, the defendant was withdrawn, silent, almost catatonic, completely uncooperative." And then, with some relish, he added: "When she did finally speak, she was abusive, hostile, and deeply distrustful."

Claudia grimaced and began drawing stick figures in her note pad. Under her breath, she whispered to Levinsky, "He didn't like my jokes."

Morrison went on. "She also has a tendency toward inappropriate humor."

Claudia gave Levinsky a what-did-I-tell-you glance, but said nothing. As for Levinsky, he was trying to ignore Claudia's asides, hoping that if he did, they might stop. He hoped Judge Murdoch might have a hearing problem of some sort, but unfortunately the man appeared to be perfectly capable of picking up on the slightest noise in his courtroom.

Over by the witness stand, MacMillan was pacing in what Kreiglitz and Levinsky were fond of calling his Perry Mason walk. "Based on your examination," he asked Morrison, "do you believe that the defendant can consult rationally with her counsel and assist in her defense?"

Morrison shook his head sadly. "No, I don't believe so."

The judge leaned over the bench and looked at Morrison. "Does this mean she can't understand the charge?"

"In this patient's case," Morrison said, "she's so convinced that the district attorney and her parents and even I are conspiring to put her away, instead of letting her stand trial, that I don't see how she could distinguish between a criminal charge and persecution."

Suddenly, Claudia sprang to her feet and called out, "I can tell the difference. *This* is persecution."

Levinsky wanted to crawl under the table and die. But before he could do that, the judge glared at him and said, "Mr. Levinsky . . ."

Nodding to indicate that he had perfect control over his client—which he knew was the absolute furthest thing from the truth—Levinsky dragged Claudia back down to her seat, and then said, "I'm sorry, your honor, it won't happen again."

Claudia sulked. For a moment Levinsky eyed her. Didn't she understand how she was making herself look by screaming about people persecuting her? He leaned over to her and whispered harshly in her ear. "Do you want to lose this?"

"It *is* persecution," Claudia shot back. "What would *you* call it?"

Levinsky sighed. "I'd call it suicide," he said honestly.

Claudia didn't seem to catch the implication that she was digging her own grave. She sat upright in her chair, her eyes flashing, as the judge said, "You may continue, Mr. MacMillan."

"Doctor," MacMillan began, "do you believe the patient is dangerous to herself and others?"

Morrison thought for a moment, then nodded and said, "Yes I do."

Once again, Claudia jumped to her feet. This time, Levinsky was prepared for the move and tried instantly to bring her back to her seat, but she struggled to remain upright and shouted out, "Define dangerous!"

Ignoring her, Morrison calmly continued. "When a patient is paranoid, and I found the patient to be paranoid—"

Claudia whirled to Levinsky. "Ask him to define dangerous," she insisted.

Levinsky, still trying to pull her to a sitting position, gave her a furious look and said, "Shut up."

Morrison tried to go on. "When someone has this patient's history, I'd consider such a patient dangerous."

"Define paranoid!" Claudia screamed.

With every bit of strength he had in him, which wasn't all that much, Levinsky yanked at Claudia as he yelled out, *"Siddown!"*

Claudia banged down into her chair with a great deal of ire. Her eyes gleamed furiously at Levinsky, whose eyes were gleaming back at her even more furiously. He tried to hold onto her, keep her pinned in her seat, but she shoved him away with disgust, as though he was deliberately sabotaging her efforts to get herself declared sane.

"Mr. Levinsky!" the judge called out disapprovingly. "If this proceeding is too much of a hardship for the defendant, I'll be happy to consider a request for an adjournment."

Levinsky turned to Claudia and eyed her questioningly. She raised an eyebrow but said nothing. So what was Levinsky to do? He stared at her with an expression that clearly stated the choice of adjournment was hers. She ignored his stare for a time, then at last seemed to relax and lean back in her chair.

"It won't be necessary, your honor," Levinsky finally said. And then he added, as contritely as he could, "I'm sorry."

But the judge was of the old school. He didn't want outbursts followed by apologies. He wanted a calm, respectable courtroom. With utter seriousness, he said, "We allow a good deal of leeway in these circumstances, Mr. Levinsky. We are not so formal here as in other courts, but I'd like to remind you that the rules of contempt apply. Does the defendant understand that?"

Claudia looked down at the table.

The judge gazed at her. "Young lady, do you understand what I just said?"

"This young lady understands what you just said," Claudia muttered sarcastically.

Levinsky tried to make peace. He knew that Judge Murdoch needed respect the way other people needed air. As respectfully as he could, Levinsky said, "She understands perfectly, your honor."

The judge looked around the courtroom for a time. He seemed to be considering whether he was feeling especially charitable or benevolent that day. Apparently, he was, for after a while, he sighed and said, "You may continue, Mr. MacMillan."

MacMillan glanced over at Claudia, who was still looking down at her table, then turned to Morrison and quietly said, "Define paranoid, doctor."

Claudia's eyes shot upward. She smiled at MacMillan, even smiled at Levinsky. But Levinsky pretended not to see her smile. He was still furious with her and didn't want to encourage any more outbreaks that would probably result not only in her case being thrown out the window, but his career along with it.

Morrison said, "A paranoid state is a mental condition in which the patient believes that people are against him. Sometimes some people. Sometimes all people. Because of this belief, the patient feels continuously threatened. And when a patient feels threatened all the time, he's likely to act out his—in this case her—violent impulses against all those supposed enemies."

Levinsky, almost unwillingly, leaned over to Claudia and whispered in her ear, "You happy now?"

Claudia shrugged sheepishly, but she quite plainly was.

"In your professional opinion, Dr. Morrison," MacMillan asked, "can the defendant be treated successfully?"

Without batting an eye, Morrison said, "Good God, yes." Then he looked at Claudia and inclined his chin toward her as though he were addressing her rather than MacMillan. "She's a perfect candidate for treatment. She's intelligent, she's not insensitive, and—most important—she's not beyond help."

Claudia rolled her eyes and leaned over to Levinsky. "Not beyond help, he says. Three weeks ago I was having a drink at the Algonquin, I saw the Matisse exhibit at the Metropolitan Museum, my pharmaceutical stock went up four and half points."

"Good," Levinsky said, grimacing. "Keep it to yourself."

MacMillan paced some more before the witness stand. Jesus, Levinsky thought, does the guy think there are TV cameras in here? He's going to get an Emmy nomination for his ability to look the part of a top-notch attorney. Levinsky grew dizzy watching MacMillan march feverishly to and fro, so he tried to keep his gaze steady on the front of the courtroom, hoping Claudia would emulate his attentiveness and silence.

"Doctor," MacMillan said while walking, "as a professional, would you like to see the defendant receive treatment before she's brought to trial?"

Morrison gave Claudia a concerned glance and nodded. "Absolutely. If she had appendicitis or pneumonia, no court in the land would expect her to go to trial; they'd postpone until she recovered. "We're not in the Dark Ages anymore; we know there are diseases of the mind as well as the body. If you put this patient under the right kind of care, she can be treated to the point where she can go to trial."

Levinsky tapped a pencil against the table. Morrison's argument was perfect: logical, sensible, and impressively stated. Without a psychiatrist as well spoken, it would be hard to refute his line of reasoning.

MacMillan seemed pleased, too. He began to wrap up. "Dr. Morrison, can you say with reasonable medical certainty that the defendant, Claudia Draper, as a result of a mental disease or defect, lacks the capacity to understand the charge against her, or to assist in her own defense?"

Morrison cleared his throat and said, "In my

professional opinion, the patient does not have the capacity to understand the charge against her, nor can she assist in her own defense."

MacMillan smiled. "Thank you, doctor." And then to Judge Murdoch: "No further questions, your honor."

The judge turned to the defendant's table: "Mr. Levinsky?"

Levinsky rose, gave a quick look of warning to Claudia, then went over to the witness stand. "If you don't mind," he told the judge, "I'm going to go rather slowly and—"

Judge Murdoch immediately cut him off. "I *mind*, Mr. Levinsky. This is a hearing, not a trial."

Oh great, Levinsky thought. I'm up here two seconds and already it's breaking the guy's ass just to let me have a chance to lose this case with some self-respect left. And to make matters worse, I've got MacMillan grinning at me.

Levinsky smiled agreeably at the judge, then turned to Morrison. He would take whatever time he had to and hope the judge didn't grow too impatient. "Dr. Morrison," he began, "you described the defendant as abusive, hostile, and deeply distrustful."

Morrison started to open his mouth to reply when Claudia called out, "And with a tendency toward inappropriate humor."

Quickly, before the judge could intervene, Levinsky glanced at Claudia and said, "Thank you." Then he spun back to Morrison. "Doctor, did you describe the defendant as abusive and distrustful?"

"Yes."

"Abusive and distrustful to whom, doctor?"

Morrison thought for a moment, crossed his leg, then said, "Well . . . the world in general."

Levinsky walked closer to the witness stand. "Yes, but the world in general was not in the room with her, you were."

With a mildly hostile glance at Levinsky, Morrison said, "And after me, Dr. Arantes."

Furrowing her brow, and speaking in a thick, deep voice, Claudia imitated Dr. Arantes for the courtroom's pleasure. *"Buenas noches, señorita, como esta?"*

Some of the spectators began to chuckle, but the judge silenced them with a deadly look and said sternly to Levinsky, "Control your client."

Levinsky ran over to the defendant's table, but Claudia hadn't finished her say. "The man couldn't speak English!" she shouted to the judge.

Taking Claudia's arm firmly, Levinsky glared and whispered to her menacingly, "I've asked two questions. You've interrupted twice. Shut the fuck up."

Claudia whispered back, "I never understood a word Arantes said."

Levinsky shook his head in despair. "You never understand a word *I* say."

The judge pointed a finger toward Claudia. "Young lady," he said, "you have been warned."

Claudia gave the judge an impertinent stare. He peered over his bifocals at her, and boldly stared back until Claudia turned meekly away and went back to doodling on her pad of paper. She drew stick figure after stick figure, connecting them like paper dolls.

With an apologetic glance at Judge Murdoch, Levinsky went back over to the witness stand.

"Dr. Arantes speaks with an accent," Morrison told Levinsky. "But he is fully qualified." And then, with inspiration: "After all, Dr. Freud had an accent."

Levinsky controlled an impulse to roll his eyes and proceeded with his questioning. "Tell me, doctor, did you ever see the defendant try to injure herself or anyone else?"

"No, not *personally*," Morrison said significantly, glancing around him to see how many people appeared to be famillиar with Claudia's attack in the courtroom the week before. MacMillan grinned, the Kirks looked away, and the judge—who knew nothing of the attack—merely tapped his fingers impatiently.

Levinsky went on. "Did you ever hear her threaten to hurt herself or anybody else."

Morrison thought about this for a moment, then reluctantly shook his head. "No," he admitted.

Now we're cooking with gas, Levinsky thought. Out loud he said, "Did *anybody* at New York County Prison Hospital ever see her hurt herself or anybody else, or threaten to hurt herself or anybody else?"

"Well, let me see," Morrison said, and began flipping through his file on Claudia. His fingers moved nervously through page after page of paper. The relaxed confidence that he had shown under questioning by MacMillan was leaving him now under questioning by Levinsky. The pages in his file slipped this way and that as Morrison looked frantically for a report by a nurse or an attendant of some misconduct on Claudia's part.

Levinsky sensed Morrison's confusion and tried to play it up. He moved closer to him and sarcastically said, "Take your time, doctor."

"I will," Morrison assured him, but he continued to move his hands frantically through his reports while Levinsky hummed low enough so that only Morrison could hear him.

Morrison looked up from his file at last. He shook his head. "I don't see a notation to that effect." And then he added hopefully, "Of course, it might not have been reported."

Levinsky looked askance at the man. "But," he said, "as far as you know, the defendant has never threatened or harmed anyone, right?"

Shifting uneasily in his chair, Morrison tried to change the subject. "She's charged with first-degree manslaughter," he said.

Levinsky started to smile. He knew he had won his point in this round and that the judge was aware of this. He also knew that he was rattling Morrison, taking the doctor out of his black-and-white world, leading him to question his own thinking. When an attorney could bring a witness to question his own thought processes, he was halfway home. If a witness could be led into seeing gray areas, the witness ceased to sound convincing to a judge.

So Levinsky was beginning to relax, to move forward with confidence in his questioning of Morrison, and was envisioning home plate at last, when suddenly Claudia, indignant about Morrison's reference to manslaughter, yelled out, "Actually, it was more like womenslaughter, only I finished first."

Levinsky whirled around. His face went ashen. Claudia sat, cocky and pleased with herself, seemingly unaware that she had just ruined her big break. What was it with her?

Judge Murdoch glared at her. "One more outburst like that and I'll have you removed from this courtroom."

Claudia glanced at the judge with an absence of expression. It was impossible for Levinsky to tell whether she knew the man meant what he said, impossible to know whether Claudia understood that she could lose her case just by making a smart-ass remark.

The judge turned toward the witness stand. "Dr. Morrison," he said, "you may continue."

Morrison had regained his composure. Self-righteously, calmly, he said, "All I know is she *did* kill a man."

Aware that he had to move quickly to get back on top with Morrison, Levinsky decided to make an appeal to Judge Murdoch's deeply conservative nature. Looking at the judge, he said, "Your honor, I know the witness is a doctor and not a lawyer, but could the court explain to him that as far as the law is concerned, the defendant is innocent."

Judge Murdoch said, "I think you've explained it well enough, Mr. Levinsky." But then he turned to the court recorder and added, "Strike 'She did kill a man.' "

Levinsky was pleased that Morrison's words were being cut from the record, but knew those words had an effect whether they were cut or not cut. Innocent until proven guilty was a remarkable concept in American law, but like all remarkable concepts, it was not at first easily grasped. Human nature, Levinsky knew, found it far easier to grasp the concept of guilty until proven innocent, which was the concept French law was based on. Human nature, unfortunately, was terribly suspicious, and Levinsky knew that his job entailed overruling the suspiciousness of human nature and trying to get people to believe that someone was sane until proven insane.

Now, Morrison was staring at Levinsky with hostility. "Very clever, Mr. Levinsky," he said, "but what you are doing with your legal tricks is depriving a sick girl of proper treatment. I want her to get better, and the only place she's going to get better is in a hospital. There is a wider context here than law. The girl has a history and you're ignoring it. A broken home, a broken marriage—"

"A broken home, a broken marriage," Levinsky mused. "Well, that's half of us."

Morrison tried to go on. "Disillusion—"

"That's the other half," Levinsky snorted.

Claudia laughed at Levinsky's quip, but MacMillan rose indignantly. "Your honor," he said, "could we eliminate Mr. Levinsky's commentary and let the doctor speak?"

The judge nodded. "Yes I agree. Go ahead, doctor."

Morrison shot Levinsky a look of superiority and went on. "We're not talking about a 'defendant.' We're talking about a very troubled patient."

Levinsky sighed. Morrison was very effectively pushing forward the idea of guilty until proven innocent. Claudia was a patient in a mental hospital, ergo she should be treated as someone who was ill. That she herself did not feel as though she should be a patient didn't enter into Morrison's equation. She was a patient, a sick person. Morrison was back into his rigid black-and-white world and he was drawing the people in the courtroom into that world.

"We're not talking about a girl from the streets," Morrison continued, "but a bright, upper-class girl who couldn't cope and broke down, a girl who became a prostitute and, in a homicidal rage, killed one of her customers."

With absolute rage at Morrison's assertions, Levinsky spun toward the judge. He couldn't have Morrison announcing Claudia's guilt before trial. "Your honor," Levinsky shouted, "I object! Nothing—"

But the judge put up his hand to silence Levinsky. This was a hearing, not a trial, and he wanted to hear everything Morrison had to say.

And what Morrison had to say was exactly what Levinsky feared most, since Morrison wanted to say things about Claudia's life-style, about her past, about her career as a prostitute, and especially about a respectable housewife cracking up and becoming a murderous call girl. "We're talking about breakdown," Morrison intoned dramatically. "*Breakdown.* When there's breakdown, it's our job to put the pieces back together. I want to tell you that's not done in a courtroom or a prison, that's done in a hospital."

Levinsky swallowed and grimaced. Morrison had opened up the can of worms just as Levinsky had feared. And now Levinsky was going to try to close the can or face a practically impossible situation of having to try to explain why Claudia had become a call girl.

So Levinsky balled up his fists and tried to move away from the prostitution issue. "Just a few questions," he said calmly to Morrison. "Did you make love to the defendant?"

Morrison stared at Levinsky as though he had just been asked if he had ever eaten mud for breakfast. "*What?*"

Levinsky smiled pleasantly. "A simple question. Did you make love to the defendant?"

"Of course not."

"Well, did she proposition you?" Levinsky asked.

Morrison shook his head, slowly catching on to Levinsky's drift. "No," he answered quietly.

Levinsky moved closer to the witness stand. "Did she touch you?"

Morrison's voice was practically a whisper. "No."

Raising his own voice, Levinsky plodded on. "Well, did she ask you for money?"

Recrossing his legs, Morrison whispered even more softly, "No."

"Did you *ask* her if she'd been a prostitute?" Levinsky demanded.

Morrison found his voice again. "Yes," he said.

"And what did she answer?"

Morrison began flipping through his file. Once more, his papers started flying about. But at last he came across the note he wanted. Quoting Claudia, he said, " 'Whoring is getting paid for work you don't want to do.' "

Levinsky pressed on. "Has the defendant been charged with prostitution?"

"I don't know," Morrison said.

"Really?" Levinsky asked. "You seem to know so much. Maybe Mr. MacMillan knows."

MacMillan stood up and, with an indulgent sigh said, "There is no charge of prostitution."

Knowing he was back on a roll, Levinsky leaned close to Morrison and pushed further. "And other than what the district attorney has told you, you have no knowledge—no personal, no professional knowledge—that the defendant ever killed anyone, either, right?"

"Well . . ." Morrison said uneasily.

Levinsky glared straight into Morrison's eyes. *"Right?"*

Morrison looked down at his files and quietly said, "Yes, that's right."

A triumphant shout came from the courtroom: "Yes, that's right!"

Levinsky turned around. There was good old Claudia, back on her feet, her eyes dancing with the thrill of victory. Quickly, Levinsky said, "I have no more questions," and then he hurried back to the defendant's table and pushed Claudia back into her chair.

Claudia was beaming happily. Deep in his heart, Levinsky was thrilled to see her so joyous, but he knew he had to contain that joy. Gruffly, he said, "Now don't start celebrating. We're still in the hole."

But there was no containing Claudia's happiness. She looked at Levinsky with a grin that almost appeared grateful. And Levinsky, against his own will, grinned back. He had pulled one out of his hat. For the time being, he had managed to get the focus off of Claudia's prostitution and her murder charge. If he could only manage to keep the focus on her behavior while in the institution, he might just be able to win the case.

MacMillan was talking with the judge. "With your permission, your honor," he was saying, "I'd like to save my redirect for later."

The judge nodded and turned to Morrison. "You can step down, doctor."

Slowly, Morrison left the witness stand. As he returned to his seat, he cast a gaze of disgust toward Claudia and Levinsky but said nothing. He had the look of a boxer who was down for a round but intended to be back. Which he would be. When MacMillan brought him to the witness stand again for a redirect, he would get his chance to launch again into the subjects Levinsky had taken away from him. And at that time there would be nothing Levinsky could do except voice objections that the judge would probably overrule.

MacMillan rose and called his next witness. "Your honor," he said, "I'd like to call Mrs. Arthur Kirk."

Suddenly, Claudia grabbed Levinsky's arm tightly. Levinsky dropped his grin and looked at her with confusion. She had never touched him before, he realized. Never accidentally even. And now she was clutching his forearm with a fierce desperation. "I don't want her up there, Levinsky," she whispered.

Levinsky shrugged. "We don't make out the invitation list."

Claudia opened her mouth, started to say something, then stopped and turned toward her mother. Her eyes, which just moments before were so full of joy, were now full of dread as she watched Rose Kirk walk nervously up to the witness stand.

Spinning back to Levinsky again, Claudia said urgently, "I don't *need* her. I don't want to *hear* her."

Something in Levinsky's mind told him that there was a significance, a kind of coded message in what Claudia was saying. He had the same feeling of Claudia trying to hide something he had had the other night. But what was it Claudia was hiding? What was she trying to keep locked inside her?

He looked at her, puzzled and curious, but she said nothing more. For a moment Levinsky was lost, unsure about whether to try to break through to whatever Claudia was keeping so tight in her or whether to allow the proceedings to continue while he and Claudia were still ahead.

At last, Levinsky decided to try to get to the bottom of things. If there was a chance Claudia might communicate with him, might explain her past to him, he needed to take it. He stood up.

"Your honor? May we have a short recess?"

Judge Murdoch looked at Levinsky with surprise, then glanced at Claudia, who was still clutching Levinsky's arm. The judge furrowed his brow, then said, "We can take a few minutes."

Claudia let go of Levinsky's arm and leaned back in her chair, obviously greatly relieved. While she sighed, the judge rose and exited from the courtroom, followed by the court recorder.

Levinsky glanced at Claudia a moment, then said, "Listen, get it through your head that it's their game and their rules. You've made it hard enough for me as it is; don't make it any harder."

But Claudia didn't seem to register his words. She seemed to be sliding into her chair, going away. She looked drained.

Trying to think of what to say next, how to begin to question her about why she was so opposed to her mother taking the stand, he turned and looked at Rose Kirk, who was near the witness chair, hesitant, obviously uncertain about whether to sit in the chair now or not.

Arthur Kirk went over to her. Levinsky watched as Kirk reached gently for his wife's trembling hand and heard him say, "Go talk to her. Tell her you love her."

Rose Kirk stared at her husband with a befuddled gaze for a moment, then, in a quavering voice said, "Come with me."

The Kirks approached the defendant's table. Levinsky thought how much they were like Jack Spratt and his wife—not because of any weight differences, but simply because they were so entirely each other's opposite: she was so diffident; he was so confident. What would it be like, Levinsky wondered, to have a diffident wife? Levinsky's wife *prided* herself on what she called her "open nature" and what Levinsky called her "open hostility." Levinsky couldn't imagine having a wife who reached tremblingly for his hand. It was far more in his wife's nature to reach furiously for his balls. Wouldn't it be nice to have a wife who was more like a puppy dog than a vulture? Or did that kind of relationship have its own problems?

Well, Levinsky realized, it was a question he would never be able to answer. He was innately incapable of attraction toward puppy-dog women.

He seemed to seek out women who treated him like garbage. His wife. Claudia. Men like Arthur Kirk wanted to be kings; Levinsky, apparently, wanted to be the joker in the deck.

Rose Kirk approached Claudia gingerly from the side. "Claudia?" she said in a whisper.

Claudia either didn't hear her mother or pretended not to hear her. She stayed with her back pressed against her chair, sunken, weary, staring straight ahead.

"Hello, darling," Rose Kirk went on. "How are you?"

Now Levinsky knew Claudia had heard her mother because her face tightened, but she kept staring straight ahead.

Rose Kirk's eyes started to fill with tears. "You look thin," she said.

At last, Claudia turned her head to the side and stared from Rose to Arthur, but she still said nothing.

Arthur Kirk moved up close to his stepdaughter. "Are they feeding you?" he asked. "I can arrange to have food sent in. Would you like that?"

Claudia gave Arthur Kirk an odd glance, but still said nothing.

Rose Kirk looked at Levinsky a moment, as though she wanted him to help her get through to her daughter. Levinsky, however, ignored her silent plea. He was watching Claudia and the Kirks with fascination, trying to determine the direction of Claudia's hostility. Was she not talking to them because they were trying to have her institutionalized? Was she more angry with one of them than the other? It was a hard situation to read.

"You look tired," Rose Kirk said after a time. "Are we making you tired? You can say so, darling."

Arthur Kirk bent down toward Claudia. "Say something, *please.*"

Claudia glared at him.

Rose Kirk tugged at her husband's sleeve. She was obviously someone who would go to any length to avoid confrontation. And the look in Claudia's eyes was extremely confrontational. "Arthur," she said delicately, "we can talk to her later." And then she gave Claudia a caring, if weak, smile and said, "We love you, dear."

All of a sudden, Claudia seemed to come to life. She moved forward in her chair, jerked her head, and said, *"What?"*

Arthur looked at her with puzzlement. "We love you," he said.

Rose let go of her husband's sleeve and came close to Claudia. "Don't you know that?" she asked tearfully.

Claudia looked down at the floor with a smile Levinsky didn't understand, and slowly said to herself, "We love you." Then she looked up at her mother and stepfather, let go of her smile, and stared at them again.

Flustered, Rose began to quiver. But her voice was strong as she said, "Yes."

Claudia looked at her mother quizzically. "We love you," she said again.

Arthur and Rose Kirk turned to each other. They didn't seem to know what to make of Claudia's words. Did she doubt their love? Didn't she understand their love?

Both of the Kirks looked at Levinsky, as though he could explain something to them. But he was as bewildered as they were. Claudia seemed to be repeating their words to them the way someone who didn't speak English might repeat the words of an American.

And then Claudia chuckled, raised her arms as if she were a conductor about to lead a choir, and said, "One more time . . . We . . . come on, we . . ."

The Kirks looked aghast, but obeyed Claudia. "We . . ." they repeated in unison.

"Love . . ." Claudia said.

"Love . . ." they repeated.

"You."

"You."

Claudia let her hands drop down and applauded. "Outstanding," she said bitterly. And then, turning quickly away from the Kirks, she said, "Let's go, Levinsky."

Levinsky signaled to Harry the Bailiff to escort Claudia to the holding pen. Harry walked up to Claudia, who walked fast and furiously toward the prisoners' entrance.

For a moment, Levinsky lingered by the Kirks.

They looked horrified, stunned. He wanted to say something to them, to comfort them, but he didn't know what words could take away their pain. So he just left them to each other and walked off after Claudia. As he exited the courtroom, he could hear Rose Kirk sobbing.

Claudia was far ahead of Levinsky, charging down the winding staircase that led to the cells. He hurried after her, knowing the time had come to confront her, but dreading what he was going to unleash in her.

SIX

Levinsky stood with his back against the door of the women's holding tank watching Claudia as she walked back and forth on the cement floor like an angry lioness in a cage at a zoo. He thought it not only courteous but wise to give her a few minutes to calm down before trying to talk to her. So he took an ancient pack of Wrigley's gum from his pocket—a birthday present from his daughter—and slowly unwrapped a stick.

At last, Claudia stopped walking and looked his way. Silently, he held up his package of gum as a peace offering, and she came over and accepted a stick, smiling even as she bit into it and became aware of how long it must have been sitting around in his pocket.

Where to begin? With the scene that had just occurred with her parents? With her silence the other night when she refused to answer his question? Or, perhaps best, with a little reassuring talk about the need for open, honest communication, between two human beings.

He started off tentatively, quietly. "You know, my wife and I—"

But Claudia broke off his speech with fury. "I don't want to hear about your wife!" she shouted.

Levinsky eyed her for a time. The last thing he wanted was to have her hysterical and explosive on the witness stand, and yet the missing link in her life was so obvious, and he had to know about it if he was to help her win her case. He didn't want to push her; he also knew if he didn't push her, MacMillan might. What to do? Just stand here like a dummy and hope she'd talk?

In a few seconds, Claudia sighed, and shook her head apologetically. "I'm sorry," she said. "Talk about your wife."

"Well," Levinsky began nervously, "I was just thinking about how people withhold . . . in a family."

Claudia gave him a curious look, as though she recognized his bait but wasn't sure if she wanted to bite. But then her look grew cooler and she not only glanced away from him, but changed the subject. "How many kids do you have?" she asked pleasantly, as if they were two people at a cocktail party not two people in a stinking, filthy prison holding tank.

Levinsky played along with her. "Three. Two boys and a girl."

Claudia looked back at him, this time with keen interest. "You going to get divorced?"

Not sure why she was asking him this but aware that his answer was somehow important to her, Levinsky decided to respond as honestly as he could. He smiled, shrugged, then said, "We talk about it . . . Then we go to the movies."

Claudia opened her mouth to ask another question, but Levinsky decided he had paid his dues: she'd asked him something painful and personal and he'd answered her truthfully; now, she could do the same for him. "Why don't you want her to testify?"

Claudia evaded him. "I just don't want her to testify."

Levinsky went over to her. "*Why*? You wouldn't let me get an independent shrink—"

Suddenly, Claudia darted away. She raced to the barred door and began banging on it. Harry the Bailiff opened it quickly.

"You can take me to my seat, officer," she said.

Harry eyed her. "No gum, Claudia."

Cheerfully and obediently, Claudia dropped her gum into a basket and followed Harry into the corridor. Levinsky remained in the tank, too upset to move, as she walked away from him. He thought of shouting out to her, but was too angry to do it without botching everything up. So instead he just slammed his fist against the concrete block wall, let the pain shoot up his arm, and screamed out a stream of words so vile that even some of the women lounging around in the tank seemed impressed. Then he realized that he was locked in the tank and cursed all over again as he stood at the bars like some guy in an old grade-B film and yelled, "Gemme outta here!"

Rose Kirk sat anxiously at the witness stand twisting a Kleenex in her fingers as MacMillan stood over her.

"Mrs. Kirk," MacMillan asked gently, "the defendant, Mrs. Draper, is your daughter, is that correct?"

Rose Kirk nodded. "Yes."

"You and your daughter's father were divorced, were you not?"

Again, Rose Kirk nodded. "Yes."

"Was it an acrimonious divorce?"

Quietly but with a cheerful determination, Rose said, "Oh no, not at all. We're civilized people. As I recall, we even wished each other luck. Now, understand, we might have exchanged a few harsh words, but other than that it was friendly."

Levinsky looked at Rose with amazement. She certainly *was* cut from a different mold than his wife. Many were the time when Mrs. Levinsky had proudly informed him that if he were ever to try to crawl out the door, she'd rake him over the coals so bad in a divorce proceeding that he'd be lucky to get out of the marriage with a pair of mismatched socks. And here was this woman, so gentle, so well bred, that she'd wished her ex-hubby *luck*? Either Rose Kirk was vying for a Nobel Peace Prize or she was not to be believed.

MacMillan continued his questioning. "And your daughter did not react badly to it?"

Rose shook her head adamantly. "She was just fine. After all, she was only five."

Again, Levinsky was shocked. He had a five-year-old daughter himself. His five-year-old had an incredible tendency to react badly to *anything* that didn't go just the way she wanted it. Being served green beans was a perfectly good reason for her to go absolutely bonkers. He presumed that such an event as divorce would throw her for quite a loop. And could Claudia—perhaps the most temperamental woman Levinsky had ever known—have been so calm and accepting as a five-year-old as to have reacted "fine" to her parents' divorce?

Levinsky glanced sideways at Claudia to note her reaction. But her face was a mask. She was listening attentively, but utterly unemotionally.

MacMillan went on. "And how soon after your divorce did you marry Mr. Kirk?"

"Eleven months," Rose said. "Nearly a year."

"And how did your daughter get along with Mr. Kirk?"

Rose smiled as though she was reliving a much better time. "Oh, fine. It was love at first sight for both of them."

Levinsky shot Claudia another glance. But still her face remained a mask.

"Mrs. Kirk," MacMillan said softly, "can you tell us when you first noticed any changes in her behavior?"

Rose looked anxiously toward Claudia, then said, "As early as the sixth grade, she was around eleven. She had been very active in school, in sports and clubs and that sort of thing. She was always a very happy child. Then all of a sudden she withdrew. She seemed to live in a fantasy most of the time."

This was all news to Levinsky, who had been under the impression that Claudia had been some kind of perfect human specimen up until the time of her divorce. He leaned forward at the table and began to listen avidly, ready to write down anything Rose Kirk said that might lead him to a new line of thinking.

MacMillan frowned and said, "You never knew how Claudia was going to act, is that it?"

Rose nodded vigorously. "Never. One day she would talk a blue streak of utter nonsense and the next day you couldn't get a word out of her. Later, in high school, we had some problems with marijuana, staying out all night, and there was a period of . . . promiscuity."

For a time, Rose looked down at the floor, but it was obvious to everyone in the courtroom she hadn't finished. Levinsky wrote down on his legal pad: *Moodiness, dope smoking, sex—if that's mental illness, then ninety percent of all teenagers should be locked up. Mother hiding something more?*

At last Rose went on timidly, still gazing down at the floor. "One night, she was sixteen . . . Arthur—Mr. Kirk—and I found her standing at the mirror in the bathroom. She had cut off all her hair. When we tried to approach her, she . . . brandished the scissors at us."

Levinsky slowly scratched out what he had written on his legal pad and now wrote two single words: *Hair—why?* He looked at Claudia. Her body was tensing up. She curled her fingers into tight fists, clenched her jaw, and pulled her shoulders in close to her. But at least she remained silent.

MacMillan, Levinsky knew, was going to go to town with this disclosure of violent behavior. He went close to Rose and said, "She turned the scissors on you as though she was going to attack you? Did you get any professional counseling?"

Immediately, Levinsky jumped to his feet. "Objection," he called out. "Prosecution is leading the witness."

Judge Murdoch thought this over, then said, "Sustained."

Rose looked up anxiously at MacMillan. Not seeming to realize that she no longer needed to answer the question about counseling, she said, "We were against that. We don't believe in airing family problems. We just assumed it was part of adolescence."

MacMillan opened his eyes wide with disbelief. "*Brandishing* a scissors on her mother and father?" He shook his head slowly, as though he couldn't fathom a more vicious act, then said with great concern, "Mrs. Kirk, do you have any idea what caused her behavior?"

Levinsky eyed Rose Kirk's face carefully. What he saw was a woman struggling deep inside herself for an answer she either couldn't—or perhaps didn't dare to?—find. At last she whispered, "I don't know." And then, looking at Claudia and speaking in her full voice, "I don't know. I know I made mistakes. Every mother makes mistakes; I'm sure I made them sometimes, but not enough times for her to carry on the way she did. Not enough times for her to drink and lie and cut school and not talk to me and not kiss me and not touch me. Not enough times for *that.*"

Now, Rose began to sob. Taking another tissue from her purse, she wiped her eyes, shook her head, and murmured, "I don't know . . . I don't know."

Levinsky looked from Claudia's tense, balled-up fists to her face. "Hold on," he whispered.

Claudia gave a slight, jerky nod, then she said, more to herself than Levinsky, "Poor Mama."

Meanwhile, up at the witness stand, MacMillan was trying to help Rose compose herself. He placed his hand on her shoulder as she continued to weep, and gently said, "Mrs. Kirk?"

The judge leaned over his bench. "Would you like to take a minute?" he asked Rose. "We can. It's quite allowable."

But Rose shook her head. "I'm all right."

And so MacMillan went on. "Claudia got married while she was still in college, didn't she?"

Suddenly, Claudia unclenched her fists. Levinsky watched from the corner of his eye as she reached for her note pad and began doodling in it with thick, heavy strokes. She made three stick figures, one with its head smaller than the others. Carefully, she gave each of the stick figures eyes and noses but not, Levinsky noticed, mouths.

Rose was talking about Claudia's marriage. "She

sent a clipping from the college paper. That's how we heard. Not even a note. *Nothing.* It hurt me terribly. And Arthur, too. She's our only child."

Levinsky wrote down, *Didn't tell mother about marriage. Doesn't want to talk to mother now. Doesn't want mother talking on witness stand. Doesn't want to talk to psychiatrists. Doesn't want to talk to me. No talking, please . . .*

Rose sighed. "I don't know what happened. When she was a little girl, she loved me so much. She used to say to me, 'I love you to the moon and down again and around the world and back again.' And I would answer, 'I love you to the sun and down again and around the stars and back again.' "

Setting his pen down, Levinsky looked over at Claudia's stick figures again. No mouths. He glanced up at Claudia's own mouth. Her lips were moving in sync with her mother's, mouthing the same rhyme as her mother, but no noise came from her mouth. Just lips moving soundlessly and her eyes staring at Rose . . .

I love you to the moon and down again and around the world and back again, and I love you to the sun and down again and around the stars and back again, but what does that mean when I am eleven years old and sitting on my bed in my pajamas sobbing and I hear your footsteps tap-tap-tapping in your high heels? You come to my door with a Scotch in your hands. I know you hear me crying because I can see your eyes through a crack in the door watching me. But why don't you come in? Why doesn't your love bring you in? Your ice cubes rattle in your glass, your high heels tap-tap-tap away from me, and then I hear your bedroom door slam. Is your love on its journey to the stars and the moon? I am waiting here in the darkness for its magical return, but night after night, no matter how hard I cry, it never comes to me. . . .

"I love you to the sun and down again and around the stars and back again," Rose Kirk said again, and then, as if she could sense how far away her daughter's stare was taking her, she cried out, "Do you remember, Claudia?"

Claudia quickly blinked and looked down at the doodles on her note pad. Quietly, she said, "Just answer the questions, Mama."

MacMillan continued. "Did Claudia get in touch when her marriage failed?"

Rose shook her head. "I found out from a friend. And I called and I said is it true? And she said, yes, it's true. And there was a big silence. So I said, come home. Stay with us till you feel better. No, she said. Just no."

Rose looked at MacMillan with fearful eyes. "I was afraid for her," she said softly. "A divorced woman is a target, she can fall prey to any polite man who comes along."

Listening keenly, Levinsky suddenly began writing down what Rose Kirk had just said about a divorced woman. Was there some connection between Rose's comment and something that had happened to the woman during the time she was divorced? Levinsky couldn't begin to sort out a firm pattern, but two things were becoming apparent to him. The words *divorce* and *love* had special significance for both Claudia and her mother.

"Were you able to keep in touch with Claudia after her divorce?" MacMillan asked Rose.

Rose sighed and rubbed one of her nervous hands across the purse on her lap. "I called and called but she never answered my messages. So instead of calling, I wrote . . . I wrote—"

Suddenly, Rose broke off speaking and grabbed her purse. She unfastened it hurriedly and pulled out from it a three-inch stack of letters tied securely with a pretty pink ribbon. Holding the letters so that everyone in the courtroom could see them, Rose said, "These are the letters. Right here. I thought you should see them because they're marked, you see?" And she waved them before MacMillan, who looked at them politely. "See? All of them, every single one, in exactly the same way."

Oy vey, Levinsky thought. We're going to have to listen to Rose Kirk read her letters to her daughter now? He stood up and turned to Judge Murdoch. "Your honor, is all this pertinent?"

But before the judge could answer, Rose turned angrily toward Claudia and pointed the letters at her daughter accusingly. "Is this your handwriting?" she demanded. "Answer me! Is this your handwriting?"

Claudia looked away.

"Is this your 'addressee unknown'?" Rose shouted out. " 'Addressee unknown.' 'Addressee unknown.' 'Addressee unknown'? There are thirty-one letters in my hand and they are all, every single one, marked 'addressee unknown'!"

For a moment, Rose waited for a response from Claudia, but when one didn't come, she furiously hurled the letters at her daughter. The pretty pink ribbon burst from them in the air and the letters went sailing, scattering, every which way in the courtroom.

Claudia slid out of her chair and began to kneel to retrieve the letters, but Levinsky took her arm and held her back. Instead, Harry the Bailiff quietly scooped them all up and handed them to MacMillan.

Judge Murdoch peered over his bifocals at Rose. "Are you sure you wouldn't like to take a short break, Mrs. Kirk?" he asked gently.

"I'm fine," Rose said, "I'm fine."

MacMillan stood to the side of the witness stand and gave Rose some time to pull herself together. She closed her purse, set it demurely back on her lap, patted the tears of rage and anguish neatly from her face, and then nodded to the district attorney that her well-bred self was in one piece again.

After clearing his throat, MacMillan continued with his questioning. "In other words," he said, as if the hearing were moving along beautifully and Rose's wild letter throwing had never occurred, "your daughter has continuously and progressively withdrawn from you for nearly twenty years. Is that right?"

Levinsky sighed. MacMillan should have been a

ventriloquist, not a lawyer. The guy had an incredible gift for putting words in witnesses' mouths.

And Rose Kirk accepted MacMillan's words with a polite nod of her head. "Yes, that's right."

MacMillan went around to the front of the witness stand. "Mrs. Kirk," he asked, "do you believe your daughter needs psychiatric help?"

Immediately, Levinsky came to his feet. "Objection! Is Mrs. Kirk a medical expert?"

Judge Murdoch raised an eyebrow, then said, "Sustained."

"I'll rephrase," MacMillan said, shooting Levinsky a fast, just-wait-till-it's-your-turn look. "As a parent, solely as a parent, would you like your daughter, Claudia Faith, to receive psychiatric treatment?"

Claudia rolled her eyes, not only at the question, but also at the use of her full name. "I'm an adult," she said loudly enough for the entire courtroom to hear. "What does it matter what she thinks?"

Judge Murdoch lifted up his gavel and banged it so that it echoed.

"It's my life, Stanley!" Claudia yelled at him.

Oh my God, Levinsky thought. Murdoch's wife probably doesn't even get to call him Stanley. Now it's all over, all down the toilet.

The judge glared at Claudia. "You're trying my patience, young lady!"

But Claudia didn't seem to care. She raised her arms, palms up, toward the judge, and came to her feet. "Why do you listen to all this?" she demanded. "Why don't you listen to me?"

"Sit down, young lady," the judge commanded. And then, setting his gavel back in place as though he feared if he didn't he might toss it at Claudia's head, he added, "You'll have your chance to testify."

Really? Levinsky thought. You mean the party's not over and we don't all have to go home?

Stunned by his good fortune, Levinsky's mouth dropped open for a second. Then he made a fast recovery and yanked Claudia firmly back into her chair. She glared at him, apparently unaware that a miracle had just occurred.

MacMillan tried to move on. "Mrs. Kirk?"

Rose looked at him, obviously puzzled. "I'm sorry. What was the question?"

MacMillian turned to the court recorder and nodded. The woman read from a sheet: " 'As a parent, solely as a parent, would you like your daughter, Claudia Faith, to receive psychiatric treatment?' "

Shifting uneasily in her chair, Rose gave a glance toward her husband, and then said, "She needs help. Yes. It's hard to say that about your own family, but yes." And then she looked at Claudia, her eyes asking for forgiveness. "I'm sorry, darling, yes."

Claudia shifted her gaze to the floor as her mother sighed and whispered, "She needs help."

Obviously pleased, MacMillan began to do his Perry Mason walk again. "Mrs. Kirk," he said, "I have one last question—"

But Rose cut him off. Turning back and forth from the daughter who wouldn't look at her to the strutting district attorney, she said, "It's not her fault. When they told me what she did, when they told me about the . . . men . . . I knew it couldn't be her fault. She couldn't do that and be in her right mind. She only loved one man in her life, her husband, Peter."

Claudia glanced up from the floor with a peculiar smile on her face. "Like you, Mama?" she asked.

"He lied!" Rose shouted out passionately. "Your real father was a *liar*. 'Rose,' he said, 'I love you, I love you more than life itself. I'll never look at another woman, there are no other women, there'll never be anyone else.' Do you know why there were? Do you have any idea? He never loved me, darling, never."

"He loved you, Mama," Claudia said quietly, her eyes turning back down toward the courtroom floor, her mind moving away . . .

They love you. You love them. You love me. I love you. Mama loves me and I love Mama and Daddy loves me and I love Daddy and Daddy loves Mama and Mama loves Daddy and Peter loves . . . Yes, Peter loved me. "I love you," he said, his voice in the beginning so deep in my heart I thought I'd faint when he first said the words. Like Romeo and Juliet, like Anthony and Cleopatra, like Nancy and Ronnie Reagan, like Mickey and Minnie Mouse. Great love, true love. Oh, but I knew even then, even as my heart was soaring, rushing with his passionate declaration, I knew all about love . . . Peter turned to me. His handsome face, his gentle eyes, his oh-so-in-love smile. "Marry me, Claudia," he said. I wanted to slap his face or kiss him or maybe I wanted to do both. We were dancing, two dumb college kids at a New Year's Eve party. Snow falling. Balloons and glitter blowers everywhere. The music so soft, so full of promises. Peter's hand on my shoulder, spinning me around the floor. Marry him? "Sounds like a lousy idea," I said. He stopped dancing. His eyes so hurt. His warm hand holding me tight. "But I love you. I'm crazy about you," he said. Well, baby, darling, sugar pops, honey bunch, sweetie pie, I was crazy about you, too. It's just that I knew better. And I tried to tell you, Peter. I tried to show you how it was with love. "Oh, that'll pass," I said, "it's like a hard-on. Marry somebody else, then I can be the other woman and I'll know where I stand." But Peter was so innocent then. "I don't want to marry anyone else," he insisted. "I want you." Oh, and it hurt to hear that, knowing years and years from then I would look back and remember how pretty it had all been that night when we believed we were gonna be different than all the other beings on this sad planet. Oh, we weren't going to lie and cheat and betray and lust and fondle and sneak and all the other crap people do to those they love ever so deeply. I thought of our marriage to come. The little house. The white picket fence. The babies. The betrayals. I said, "What do I get for it, Peter? A stove and a refrigerator?" Oh, he thought I was just embarrassed, just being a smart-ass. He held me closer on the dance floor. He wanted to twirl my cynicism away. His fingers pressed against my back, begging me to trust him forever and ever. He sang along with the record on the stereo: "A love whose burning light will warm the winter night, that's all, that's all." Oh, and

God I knew better, knew so much better than he did, but what the hell was I supposed to do? I loved him. I was crazy about him. So why not marry him and see how many anniversaries it would take to rip each other's hearts to shreds?

Levinsky could hear Claudia humming an old love song from the late 1960s. He gave her a curious glance and tapped her on the shoulder. She instantly stopped humming and looked straight ahead at her mother.

"Mrs. Kirk," MacMillan asked, "do you love your daughter?"

Rose nodded earnestly.

The court recorder glanced at the judge. "Can she say it for the record?"

"I love my daughter," Rose said.

MacMillan looked around the courtroom, then turned to Rose with a pleased expression on his face. "Thank you, Mrs. Kirk." And to Judge Murdoch: "I have no further questions, your honor."

With a relaxed and confident stride, MacMillan returned to his seat as Levinsky leaned over to Claudia and asked, "All true?"

"Close enough," Claudia replied. And then she took hold of Levinsky's jacket sleeve. Looking into his eyes, she whispered urgently, "Let her go."

Levinsky grimaced and said nothing.

"Mr. Levinsky," the judge called out, "do you have any questions?"

Giving Claudia a quick glance, Levinsky rose and walked slowly over to the witness stand. He could still see Claudia's eyes, so desperate for him to leave her mother alone, but he had to cut through Rose Kirk's testimony or Claudia would lose her case. MacMillan had succeeded in creating an image of Claudia as someone whose own mother thought she had been the victim of mental illness since the age of eleven. Testimony like that couldn't be allowed to stand unchallenged in a sanity hearing.

Levinsky stood at a distance from Rose, looked at the woman's sad face and trembling hands for a moment, and then asked, "Mrs. Kirk, would you like to take a minute?"

Rose shook her head no.

So Levinsky squared his shoulders and began what he felt he had to begin: "Mrs. Kirk, you said that you and the defendant's father—"

Suddenly, Claudia rapped the defendant's table with a water glass. Levinsky heard the noise, spun around, and saw her action for what it was: a protest. But what the hell was he supposed to do? He had to begin peeling away at Rose Kirk like an onion and see if the woman was holding back something that would help rationally explain the episodes of violence and seeming madness in Claudia's past.

Levinsky went on. "You testified that when the defendant was in high school—"

Again, Claudia banged down her water glass, this time harder. When Levinsky spun around to her, she shook her head at him with anger.

Turning to the judge, Levinsky asked, "May I have a moment, your honor?"

Judge Murdoch nodded wearily.

Levinsky ran over to Claudia. She was clasping her glass, a look of mulelike stubbornness on her face.

"What?" Levinsky asked her.

By way of reply, Claudia banged her glass once more.

Exasperated with her silence, Levinsky shoved a hand through his unruly hair and said, "You have to let me discredit the witness against you."

Again, Claudia banged down her glass.

Levinsky felt like smashing the glass against the courtroom wall. Here he had an opportunity to help Claudia, and she was doing her best to thwart him. What was he supposed to do if she wouldn't speak to him, wouldn't even let him speak to the witnesses who were being used against her? He felt like he was swimming with his hands tied behind his back. If he couldn't do a cross-examination of Rose Kirk, he was going to sink.

Claudia was looking at Levinsky with a plea in her eyes for him to let her mother go. He tried to match that plea with his own determination to win the case at any cost, but the plea got to him as a man, hit a part of himself that wasn't just a lawyer but was a mushy human being. And so, knowing he was painting himself in a corner, knowing he was being a crummy lawyer, he turned around to the judge and said quietly, "Your honor, I have no more questions." And then he sank into the chair next to Claudia, silently calling himself a sucker, an idiot, a wimp, and, of course, a schlemiel.

The judge gave Levinsky a glance of surprise, then leaned over the bench toward Rose and said, "You may step down, Mrs. Kirk."

Slowly, Rose stood up and tentatively made her way back to her seat. Levinsky watched her pass. She looked so lost, so weak. It was hard to believe that only minutes before she had been slamming a packet of pink-ribboned letters at her daughter's head. Levinsky wished he'd had the chance to explore the anger in Rose that had made her throw those letters. Every instinct in him told him that the woman was hiding something, something Claudia knew about and wanted to keep hidden. If Rose Kirk truly thought her daughter was mentally ill, she wouldn't be so furious with her. And if Claudia wasn't trying to keep something secret, she wouldn't be adamant about getting her mother off the witness stand. There had to be something between these two: something that made both of them violent. But how was Levinsky ever to find it if he couldn't speak to the woman?

MacMillan was walking toward the bench, obviously pleased that Rose Kirk wasn't going to be cross-examined. Even Perry Mason was never *that* lucky.

"I call Arthur Kirk," MacMillan said.

Claudia's stepfather headed toward the witness stand as though he were moving toward an executive conference room. He walked steadily, his arms swinging confidently. Halfway to the stand, he met up with his wife and gave her a tender embrace that showed both his concern for the ordeal she had been through and his confidence that everything was going to be just fine. Then he moved on, nodding to the judge and MacMillan the way one might to business partners, and stood by the witness seat.

Harry the Bailiff went over to him. "Do you solemnly swear the testimony that you shall give in this special proceeding shall be the truth, the whole truth, and nothing but the truth?"

"I do," Arthur said solemnly.

"Be seated."

Arthur sat down in a relaxed, yet expectant pose. He seemed to take over the witness stand in a way his wife hadn't. There was an expansiveness in his demeanor, a comfortable attitude, as though he knew as much about being a witness as he did about being an executive.

MacMillan approached him with a smile, and Arthur smiled back. Over at the defendant's table, Levinsky shook his head. He couldn't stand the mutually congratulatory attitudes successful men brought to their dealings with each other—the slap on the back, the gin and tonic delivered with a hearty chuckle, the didn't-we-go-to-the-same-prep-school invitations to each other's country clubs. If Levinsky were a success—which he recognized as an unlikely possibility—he would give his wife permission to shoot him if she ever saw him engaging in such BS.

"Mr. Kirk," MacMillan began, "how old was the defendant when you married her mother?"

Arthur thought for a moment, then said, "Claudia was five."

"At that time, was there anything about her that would have led you to believe that Claudia was troubled?"

"She was frightened," Arthur said decisively. "They were both frightened when I first met them. They'd been abandoned, you see. By Claudia's natural father."

Levinsky stared curiously at Arthur's face. There was something pleased in the man's eyes as he recounted the fear Rose and Claudia had felt, and how he had come on the scene as a rescuer of damsels in distress. A lot of men, Levinsky knew, liked to play the knight in shining armor, and obviously Kirk was one of those men; he was the big strong guy who could scare away the bogey man. But somehow, all these years after Rose Kirk had been rescued by her big, strong guy, she still seemed to be acting as though the bogey man was after her. Why, Levinsky wondered, was Rose Kirk still so frightened now that she had her knight in shining armor at her side?

Something else troubled Levinsky. Rose Kirk had made a point of insisting that Claudia was "fine" after the divorce. But Arthur was contradicting his wife's testimony. On his legal pad, Levinsky wrote, *Kirk saw C. as frightened." Mrs. K saw her as "fine." Who saw the truth?*

MacMillan went on. "So you would describe Claudia as frightened, traumatized?"

"Yes, and always on guard," Arthur said, "always distrustful." But then he shook his head. "Oh, I shouldn't say *always.* There were periods when she was a delight—and happy—but they were short-lived."

Again, Levinsky turned to his legal tablet and wrote, *Mrs. K. distinctly remembers Claudia's behavior as becoming distrustful at age eleven. She's specific about that age. Kirk says she was always that way. Can a five-year-old be as deeply distrustful as he says she was? And if she was, wouldn't the mother be the one to notice that?*

"Did you get along?" MacMillan asked Arthur.

"Yes," Arthur said proudly, "We got along fine. I was her champion."

MacMillan glanced at Arthur. "What do you mean by that."

Once more, a look of pleasure came over Arthur's face as he remembered the past. "I forbade Rose to spank her. We were never spanked in my house and I believe no child should ever be spanked. It breaks the spirit."

Levinsky looked over at Claudia. Maybe she could have used a little spirit breaking. Perhaps if Arthur Kirk had spanked her once or twice, she wouldn't be such a hothead to her lawyer. . . .

"You tried to be a good father to Claudia?" MacMillan asked.

Arthur nodded. "I tried. When I was courting her mother and she said to me, 'Art, what about

Claudia Faith,' I didn't say, 'Send her to school, give her away.' No sir. I said, 'Rose, if you love her, I love her.' "

Levinsky glanced over at Claudia to see what she thought of her stepfather's testimony. Her face again seemed a mask. She was listening intently, but not letting her reactions show in her features.

Arthur went on. "When she woke up and cried in the night with bad dreams, I was the one who went to her. I didn't know very much about children, but I learned. When she got a little older, I even took her to the office with me."

MacMillan nodded and paused for a few seconds, as though he wished the courtroom to absorb Arthur Kirk's incredible fathering skills. Levinsky used the time to reflect on those skills. It seemed amazing to him that Arthur Kirk, as opposed to Rose, was the parent who had gone to Claudia's room when she was having nightmares. Levinsky's kids had an incredible craving for their mother during such times. If there was a bolt of thunder, if they had a nightmare, if they wanted a drink of water, if they fell down and hurt themselves, the first word out of their mouths was "Mommy!" If Levinsky's wife tried to have him deal with the situation, the kid would continue to scream for his wife. It sometimes hurt Levinsky's feelings, but his wife assured him it was normal for children to call out to their mothers in a crisis, not their fathers. Levinsky had believed his wife. But here was Arthur Kirk, immediately upon becoming a stepparent, being the one to calm a child's nightmare. Had Claudia called out in the night for him? Hadn't she, like Levinsky's kids, screamed "Mommy"?

Now MacMillan went on. "Given your years with Claudia, Mr. Kirk, and the close relationship you shared, would you say you understood her pretty well?"

"I think so," Arthur said. "She was a troubled but lovely child, a joy to me in spite of everything. And even though I don't have the opportunity to see her now"—and here he paused for a moment and his eyes met Claudia's—"I'm sure she's a very special woman."

"Were you surprised when her marriage collapsed?" MacMillan asked.

Levinsky stood up. If MacMillan wanted to inquire about a witness's reaction, he was supposed to ask directly, not put words into the witness's mouth. Technically, he should have asked, "How did you feel when her marriage ended?" He shouldn't have asked if the reaction was surprise. So Levinsky called out, "Objection. Leading the witness."

Judge Murdoch apparently didn't hold the same views as Levinsky about what constituted leading a witness. "Overruled," he quickly said.

Arthur Kirk answered MacMillan's question as Levinsky sat down. "All that surprised me was that the marriage lasted so long. I didn't know Peter until after they were married, and not very well then. He's a remarkable young man."

Suddenly, Claudia rolled her eyes and shouted out, "You hated him!"

Judge Murdoch slowly shook his head. "Mrs. Draper," he said, "do *not* start up again."

Claudia opened her mouth but Levinsky grabbed her arm and called apologetically to the judge, "Sorry, your honor."

But Claudia didn't appear to be very sorry. She spun toward Levinsky with flashing eyes and said, loud enough for everyone to hear, "That didn't mean anything, when he swore to tell the truth?"

Levinsky shrugged and was about to tell her to shut up when she sprang to her feet and announced to the court, "He hated Peter's guts!"

Now, Judge Murdoch's voice became sharp and threatening as he glowered at Claudia and said, "You will have your turn to speak, Mrs. Draper. Sit down."

Claudia stood for a second more. Levinsky was afraid to try to yank her down into her chair. He could see how furious she was, and suspected if he tried to grab her she might overreact. So he remained still, hoping her own desire to win her case and not get it thrown out of court by Judge Murdoch would bring her to her seat, if not her senses. And it did appear to do that. She crashed into her chair, fuming but quiet, and stared at the court recorder, as though trying to look at anyone else in the courtroom would be altogether too much for her senses. She watched the recorder's fingers tapping away at a keyboard. . . .

Tap-tap-tap-tap-tap-tap-tap. Stop tapping. Stop it and

just go away. Leave me alone. The steam rising from the tub. The water blasting into the tub. The water is almost loud enough to make the tapping go away, but not quite, never quite. And then he starts jiggling the bathroom door, wanting to come in. I stand in my robe, gripping the edge of the sink, watching the steam rise over the mirror. I like watching myself go away in the mirror. The steam is hiding me, protecting me, but the door handle keeps wiggling and the tapping gets louder. I hear his voice: "Don't do this to me again, honey. I love you." His voice is so gentle, so soft. His words sound so true that they make me cry. He doesn't believe in locked doors, he says. "I promise I'll just hold you," he tells me. Oh, but I've been promised that before, Peter. Better just to have you go away. So stop tapping. Stop begging to be let in because I'm not ever, ever, ever letting anyone in again.

Levinsky could sense that Claudia was far away, but decided to let her remain wherever her mind had taken her rather than risk another explosion at her stepfather.

MacMillan was finishing his questioning. "Speaking as a loving and devoted parent, do you believe your stepdaughter is in need of hospitalization?"

Without the slightest hesitation, Arthur said, "Yes, I'm sorry to say I do."

Smiling, MacMillan turned toward Levinsky. "I have no further questions," he said.

The judge nodded. "Mr. Levinsky?"

Levinsky glanced again at Claudia. She was still staring at the court recorder, unblinking, in some kind of trance. It troubled Levinsky to think of leaving her like that as he went to cross-examine Arthur Kirk, but he suspected if he pulled her from her thoughts, she might object—as she had objected with her mother—to his asking questions. And he was damned if he was going to let another witness get away from him. So he left Claudia as she was and walked up to the witness stand.

"Mr. Kirk," he began, "*did* you hate Peter?"

At the mention of Peter's name, Claudia quickly looked up from the court recorder and glanced at Levinsky with startled eyes. Levinsky saw her from his side. She appeared shocked to see him talking to her stepfather.

Arthur seemed equally shocked to have Levinsky asking him if he had hated his son-in-law. "No," he said, giving Levinsky a look that seemed to imply Levinsky was an utter fool to listen to the rantings of his crazy stepdaughter. But then he grinned and added, "Oh, I may have had the typical father's reaction: no man is good enough for my daughter."

Levinsky nodded. "I see." But he didn't see. Somebody was lying. Either Claudia or her stepfather. He walked over to Claudia, not only to make sure she was okay, but also to give himself a chance to formulate his next move.

Claudia glared at Levinsky. "Forget him," she said. "You're wasting your time."

Levinsky leaned toward her. "Look, you've tied my hands behind my back. At least let me walk around a little bit."

Claudia grimaced and turned away. But at least

she didn't plead with him not to question Arthur the way she had pleaded about Rose. So he turned back to the witness stand and said, "Mr. Kirk, do you know why the defendant attacked her former attorney, Clarence Middleton?"

Arthur turned his reply into a joke: "Obviously," he said with a smile, "she didn't like his advice."

Levinsky ignored the titters that followed this remark and pressed on. "And what *was* that advice?"

"I seem to recall that he suggested that a hospital was a better place for her than Riker's Island."

Levinsky cocked an eyebrow. "Really."

Arthur nodded. "He felt it was the best way."

"I see," Levinsky said. " 'The best way.' And when you and your wife talked to Dr. Morrison, when you chatted with him about the crime she'd been charged with, did he also tell you it was the best way?"

"Yes."

Levinsky walked closer to the witness stand, then stopped directly before Arthur and stared at him. "And what does that mean to you, Mr. Kirk: 'the best way'?"

Arthur Kirk gave Levinsky a what-are-you-an-idiot kind of glance, and then said, in a patient voice, "Mr. Levinsky, a trial is a public event. If she were your daughter, would you want her laughed at, hammered into a pulp by attorney's and the press? She's just a client to you—day after tomorrow you're gone—but she's not just a client to me. I'm not going to see her humilated in front of the whole world." And then he launched into one of the most self-righteous spiels Levinsky had heard since the days when he had watched *Father Knows Best.* "No, sir, this is not a common criminal. My child is ill and I'm going to do everything in my power to help her get better. And that doesn't include letting her sit in a public courtroom and be destroyed."

Unconsciously, Levinsky began to pace. As much as he knew what Arthur had said was self-serving, he also knew he risked the destruction of Claudia as a person in his defense of Claudia as a client. She didn't want him up here cross-examining her stepfather, and yet he was here. If he began to poke his nose into Claudia's past, if he were to uncover the things she was trying so desperately to keep hidden, what would become of her?

He looked her way. She wouldn't look at him, was obviously furious that he was up at the witness stand. And yet he felt obliged to go on, didn't see how he could possibly help her with her case if he didn't go on. And so he began: "Mr. Kirk, when you married Mrs. Kirk, uh . . ."

He stopped, rattled by Claudia's anger, by his own uncertainty as to how hard to push.

Judge Murdoch glanced at him uneasily. Even MacMillan stared at him. It was unusual for an attorney to cut off his own question. It showed a certain lack of professionalism, a sign that he'd lost faith in his ability to win the case.

Levinsky looked around the courtroom. He could feel himself pulled in two directions. He knew as long as he didn't decide whether his allegiance was to Claudia the client or Claudia the human being, he was not going to be of use to either Claudia. Finally, he swallowed. He was going to go all out for Claudia . . . the client.

He spun toward Arthur. With a bold, strong voice, he said, "Mr. Kirk, you and your wife were warm, caring parents, weren't you? Both of you loved the defendant."

"And we still do," Arthur said with a warm-hearted smile.

"Yes," Levinsky said. "That's why I can't quite understand why the defendant behaved the way you've described it."

Arthur shook his head sadly. "She was abandoned, her father walked out on her, she was unprotected."

"But you replaced him with something more substantial," Levinsky said keenly.

"That's right," Arthur said proudly, not evidently seeing that after a knight in shining armor rescues a damsel in distress, the damsel is supposed to stop screaming in terror.

"You replaced him with love and affection and security," Levinsky added.

The pride continued to shine on Arthur's face. "That's right."

Now Levinsky moved close to the witness stand. Frowning, he said, "Given all you gave her, that doesn't make sense, does it?"

"No, it certainly doesn't," Arthur agreed.

"Unless you gave her too much," Levinsky said

quietly. And then he stared straight into Arthur's eyes. "Maybe you were too generous," he suggested.

Arthur shifted in his chair, but his voice remained calm. "I'm not ashamed to say I was very generous. I'm a generous man."

"Do you think perhaps you spoiled her?" Levinsky asked.

"Look"—Arthur sighed—"I loved her. When you love someone, you give them things: Christmas, birthdays, graduation."

Levinsky nodded. He'd heard this line of reasoning from his own wife. If Levinsky *really* loved her, he was constantly being told, he would find a way to buy her a fur coat. . . .

Arthur went on. "When Claudia was young, I gave her presents. When she got older I gave her gift certificates. Sometimes cash."

"My mother always warned me not to give my children money," Levinsky said.

"I disagree," Arthur said with conviction. "Look, I'm a businessman, and to me running a home is just like running a business. You want somebody to do something, you give them incentive to do it."

Something about these words jarred Levinsky. He knew how it was with kids. If you asked them to take out the garbage, they'd say, "In a minute." And hours, maybe even days, could pass. Sure you could hand the kid a dollar, but then the kid would think he was taking the garbage out to earn money, as opposed to taking the garbage out because he was *supposed* to take the garbage out, because it was his *responsibility*, because it was *the right thing to do as a member of a family.* Levinsky didn't know how you developed a kid's conscience if your every transaction revolved around dollars and cents rather than right and wrong. Or was this just the way it was at Levinsky's house? Maybe only in lower-middle-class Jewish homes were kids trained by a system of guilt. Maybe in wealthier homes, money, rather than a clean conscience, was the reward for a task completed.

Arthur was describing his method of child rearing. "If Claudia straightened up her room, she got a dollar. If she did well in school and brought home a good report, she got a ten-dollar bill."

"A kind of reward system," Levinsky mused.

"Exactly. Let them have a little money, give them a sense of responsibility. Let them make their own choices.".

Levinsky stared at Arthur a moment. "And what did Claudia choose, Mr. Kirk?" he asked softly. "Didn't she choose to withdraw from you and Mrs. Kirk?"

Claudia's water glass banged down on the defendant's table with a terrific thud. But Levinsky ignored the sound and continued. "And withdraw from her husband, Peter, and from everyone else in her life."

Now, Levinsky turned and glanced at Claudia. "God knows what's left for her to withdraw from," he said pointedly, and then he went quickly over to her, leaned over the table, and said, "Listen, you can ask your stepfather one question, and he's got to answer it. What's the question?"

But Claudia wasn't biting Levinsky's bait. She gave her lawyer a sarcastic glance, and quipped, "Whatever happened to Desi Arnaz?"

Levinsky felt like slapping her, but instead he yanked her note pad from her and flipped to the page where she had drawn her stick figures. He shoved the pad close to Claudia's face. "Speak no evil, speak no evil, *speak no evil*!" he said furiously, gesturing at each of the three stick figures. "The people in your life have no mouths. What can't they talk about?"

Claudia looked away. Levinsky leaned toward her, but suddenly Judge Murdoch called out to him, "Are you through with the witness, Mr. Levinsky?"

Purple with rage, Levinsky said, "Not just yet, your honor." And then he pointed at Claudia and talked to her through gritted teeth. "Now, you can bang that goddamn glass till they take it away, but I'm going to talk to this witness."

He spun sharply back to Arthur Kirk. Still with anger in his voice, he said, "Mr. Kirk, you must be a saint. Only a saint would love a frustrating woman like this. Could you love a woman like this?"

Arthur looked at Levinsky with a shocked expression. "*What?*" he asked. "I've *always* loved her."

Levinsky walked quickly back to the witness stand. "*How* could you love her?" he asked honestly. "This is a woman even a father could hate."

Judge Murdoch leaned over the bench, and sternly said, "Mr. Levinsky . . ."

But Levinsky had had it. All this sugar-and-spice talk of love, love, love in a family where the members didn't even talk to each other. Somebody was bullshitting, and Levinsky suspected that somebody was Arthur Kirk. Gesturing toward Claudia, Levinsky said, "*This* is a woman you'd want to beat with your belt. Maybe she drove *you* crazy, too. Did *you* ever get so frustrated with her that *you* wanted to beat her?"

Arthur's jaw dropped incredulously. "Is this your idea of humor, Mr. Levinsky?"

Levinsky slammed his hand down on the witness stand. "Did you ever lose your temper with her?" he demanded.

Calmly, Arthur said, "As a parent with a child, over the years, yes, one time or another I lost my temper. And, yes, I've spanked her."

Suddenly, Levinsky smiled. At last, at long last, the bullshit was ending. He felt his own anger start to leave him as he looked curiously at Arthur and said, "You spanked her? But didn't you tell Mr. MacMillan that you *never* spanked her?"

Arthur looked uneasily from Levinsky to MacMillan, then back again. Levinsky could sense the man was starting to lose his glib confidence. And sure enough, when Arthur spoke again, it was with an edge of doubt. Gone was his absolute authority, his big, booming, business executive voice. Almost quietly he said, "Well, once or twice, maybe I spanked her." But then he began to rebuild his confidence, sat up straighter in his chair, and went on, "And I probably did a bunch of other stupid things, but I think so have most parents at one time or another. But I was always there for her. I helped her with her homework. I dressed her. I bathed her. I was the one who gave her breakfast before she went to school."

Levinsky knew Arthur was trying to reassert himself in the questioning, but he was determined not to let him gain control. Something had to be at the bottom of Claudia's behavior. If the man had lied about spanking the child, maybe he was lying about the extent of that spanking. So Levinsky pressed on. "Did you ever lose control?" he asked Arthur pointedly.

Arthur opened his mouth to respond to the question, when suddenly a voice screamed out from the back of the courtroom, *"You stop that!"*

Levinsky turned around and saw Rose Kirk, trembling now with fury, not timidity, glaring at him more angrily than her daughter had ever glared at him. But he ignored the glare, turned back to Arthur, and demanded, "Did you ever beat her?"

"Arthur Kirk would never do anything to hurt Claudia!" Rose screamed.

Levinsky spun around once more, but this time, instead of Rose's glaring eyes, he saw Claudia leap to her feet, whirl toward her mother, and cry out, "How would *you* know, Mama? You weren't there!"

Rose's mouth dropped open. She looked as though Claudia had just punched her. Slowly, she closed her mouth, her eyes riveted on her daughter.

Levinsky glanced from one woman to the other. He could feel the adrenaline rushing through him as he thought, Here we go! The stick figures were at last getting mouths.

But MacMillan was determined to block a scene. He came to his feet to voice an objection. "Your honor," he began.

Instantly, the judge waved a hand at MacMillan to silence him. He appeared as curious as Levinsky about what was to follow Claudia's disclosure.

Levinsky didn't want to lose a second. So something had happened between Claudia and her stepfather. And now he was determined to unearth it. "Excuse me, your honor," he said. "Excuse me, Mr. Kirk. May I go on, your honor?"

"Proceed," the judge said.

Arthur Kirk looked at his wife, who was still standing in the back of the courtroom. "Sit down, darling," he told her, and she obeyed.

"Mr. Kirk," Levinsky said, "you said that among the many fatherly duties you assumed when Claudia entered your life was bathing her. You did say that, didn't you?"

Uneasily, Arthur nodded. "Yes . . ."

"How long did you practice that fatherly duty?"

MacMillan bolted to his feet again. "Objection, your honor!"

But Judge Murdoch didn't even wait to hear the grounds on which the objection was based. "Overruled," he shot back quickly, and then said to Arthur, "Answer the question."

"I don't remember," Arthur said quietly.

"Well, did it stop when she was five or did it continue a year and stop when she was six—"

Arthur glowered at Levinsky. "What are you suggesting?" he asked.

But Levinsky didn't feel he had to say what he was suggesting. Arthur and every other person in the courtroom knew he was damn well suggesting child molestation. And so he continued: "—or did it go on two years and stop when she was seven?"

Arthur glanced around the courtroom as though he could find an answer someplace outside of himself. His eyes finally settled on MacMillan, but MacMillan looked away from him with embarrassment.

"You're under oath, Mr. Kirk," Levinsky reminded Arthur. "Answer the question."

"I don't know," Arthur said at last. "It didn't last long. Claudia liked me to do it."

"Do what?" Levinsky asked softly.

"To bathe her," Arthur said. And then again he looked around the room. This time he turned to Claudia, his gaze meeting hers, as he said, "It was nothing. I object to your insinuations."

Claudia stared fixedly, evenly, at her stepfather for a second, then hurriedly shifted her eyes back to the nimble fingers of the court recorder.

Tap-tap-tap-tap-tap-tap-tap. Oh go away. Please go away. Please stop knocking. Leave me alone in here. Let the steam cover me up. There. The steam is hiding me in the bathroom mirror, taking my naked body away from his tap-tap-tap.

Levinsky whirled toward Arthur. "My daughter locked me out of the bathroom when she was four. How old was Claudia?"

I'm so scared. I can't stop the tapping. Oh, and now the door handle's jiggling. He's trying to come in. But I'm not going to let him. No, I'm not going to listen. I'm going to turn my bathtub water up so high I won't be able to hear the tapping. And then I can tell him I would have let him in only I couldn't hear. Then everything will be fine. Then we'll be like other people and Mama will love me and I'll love Mama and Mama will love Daddy and Daddy will love—

"Claudia!" Arthur Kirk called out, pleading with his stepdaughter to help him explain. But Claudia was gone, lost in the time Levinsky was trying to get Arthur to talk about.

"Was she ten?" Levinsky asked. "Twelve?"

Arthur said nothing.

Levinsky turned to Claudia. He called to her, tried to bring her back. "How old, Claudia?"

I stand naked by the bathtub. How old am I? I am the age other girls receive their first kiss, their first corsage, their first touch. Other girls talk on the phone, compare notes as to how far they intend to let their boyfriends go. Me, I stand here in the bathroom trembling, goose bumps all over me, my hands covering my mouth so I won't scream. I try not to look at the door, but I do. I see a fifty-dollar bill slide along the tile on the floor; I see his hairy fingers pushing the bill beneath the door.

There was no reaching Claudia. Levinsky eyed her a moment, concerned but knowing he had to proceed, had to get to the bottom of this. He spun to Arthur: "How *old*, Mr. Kirk? Thirteen? Fourteen?"

Arthur's lips moved, but at first no sound came

out of them. When he finally did manage to speak, it was with a raspy whisper. "She was a little girl, she couldn't have been more than . . . more than—"

I climb into the bathtub, close my eyes so I don't have to see that twenty-dollar bill, clamp my hands over my ears so I don't have to hear him tapping. The hair on my head doesn't even touch my ears. I thought it would help if I made myself look like a boy, but I can't seem to do that. If only I could chop off my breasts as easily as I chopped off my hair, maybe that would stop him, but his fingers keep pushing the bill, gliding it closer to me. How old am I? Old enough to be bought. Young enough to be bought. How old?

"*I was sixteen!*" Claudia screamed, her hands covering her ears, her eyes squeezed shut.

The entire courtroom went silent. Even the recorder stopped typing for a moment. Levinsky swallowed hard. He had done it, had found what Claudia had been hiding all these years. And now there was no turning back.

He turned to Arthur. "What else occurred in that bathroom between you and your stepdaughter? What happened in her bedroom?"

Rose Kirk, half screaming, half weeping, stood up and reached out her hands. "Stop it! Stop it!"

Levinsky glanced at her for a moment, then looked furtively toward Claudia, whose eyes were scrunched up as though they would never open again, whose ears were pushed so hard against her head that her hands were white from the pressure.

I can't stop them from coming in my bathroom. They

keep coming at me. I try to hide, but they won't stop. I can see Allen Green's bloody hands trying to push his way into my bathroom. I try to close the door, try to lock him out, but he won't stop. He wants to hurt me. They say they love me but they want to hurt me. I try to slam the door closed, but I can't. I never could. Allen reaches for my neck with his bloody hands. This is how it is. First they put you in the bathtub, gently bathe you with Ivory soap and sing you songs and give you little toy ducks to bobble in the water. "Do you love Daddy?" "Yes I love you, Daddy." "How much do you love Daddy?" "I love you wider than my hands go, Daddy." Then they scoop you from the tub, rub you with a big fluffy pink towel. "Does this feel good?" "Yes, Daddy." "And does this feel good?" Very gently, they rub you. "Daddy, those are my private parts." "I know, I know. So we'll keep this private. A secret just between Daddy and his little princess. You like secrets, don't you, Claudia?" Oh, it all starts out so gentle, so soft, the pink towel between your legs. And then it starts to hurt and it doesn't stop hurting. And now, this is where it ends, with Allen Green's bloody fingers on my neck. They take away your childhood. They take away your self-respect. They take away your ability to trust, to love, to believe in anyone or anything. And then they kill you.

Arthur Kirk was looking at his wife with desperation. His face seemed shrunken, older as he called out, "It's not true, Rose, you know it's not true."

But Rose turned away from him as she began to weep loudly. She shifted her gaze to Claudia, who was moaning as she sat at her table alone, not hearing, not seeing.

Arthur, too, glanced at Claudia. His eyes looked her way hopefully, as though she might pull herself together, smile brightly, and come skipping up to her daddy. But her moaning only grew louder, her eyes only shut tighter, and at last Arthur stood up from his chair and roared to Levinsky, "You bastard! Look what you've done to her!"

"Sit down, Mr. Kirk," Judge Murdoch said sternly.

But Arthur didn't sit down. Instead, he began lumbering toward Claudia.

Suddenly, Dr. Morrison stood up. Glancing from Claudia to the judge, he called out, "Your honor, my patient needs attention. We have to get her back to the hospital."

The judge opened his mouth to reply, but Levinsky—his face covered with sweat, his eyes full of wild rage—began to chase after Arthur as he yelled: *"Answer the question, Mr. Kirk, did you make your stepdaughter your lover?"*

He's trying to strangle me, trying to take my life away from me. Well, he can have my lips, my mouth, my breasts, my vagina, but goddamm it, he's not going to have my life. I try to push him away. He throws the decanter at me. I duck, but see the mirror shatter. Everything's shattering, breaking into pieces, cracking. I'm cracking . . .

Suddenly, Judge Murdoch stood up at the bench and announced, "That's *enough,* Mr. Levinsky." And then, as Arthur continued to move toward Claudia and Levinsky continued to pursue Arthur, the judge called out, "*Adjourned.* This court is adjourned until ten o'clock in the morning." He turned and quickly exited the courtroom.

Arthur was inches from Claudia. "Baby," he begged, "tell them it's a mistake. Tell them I didn't do anything wrong."

. . . up. I'm cracking up, Mama. I sit on my little bed, only seven years old, crying for you. I'm sore. I'm so sore and so scared, Mama. Please come in my room. Please help me. But you look at me through the crack in my bedroom door and you go away and you send him in instead.

"I told her more than once I didn't want to give her a bath!" Arthur screamed out. "It was Rose's idea!"

I can hear you. You're so close to me, always so close to me. I'm seven years old. You're not supposed to be this close to me. But you push your twenty-dollar bills under my bathroom door and I turn the lock and let you in, even though my teeth chatter, even though I'm already so sore. You've been doing this to me since I was five, I don't know why it still hurts so much, but it does. Love hurts. Love hurts, you tell me. And now here you are again, trying to hurt me with your love again.

Claudia opened her eyes. Her stepfather's face was directly over hers. She whimpered as he reached for her, slid down in her chair like a small child, then crawled beneath the table.

Arthur went down on his knees. He held his hands out to her, protectively, reassuringly. In a soothing voice he whispered, "Tell them it isn't true, darlin'. For your mother's sake, take it back."

Claudia's eyes went wide with fear and she began to shake her head, at first slowly, then faster and faster.

Turning around to the courtroom, Arthur cried out, "Don't you see she's not in her right mind?"

He comes toward me with the pink towel. I walk backward but he follows after me, smiling. He wraps the towel around me, so fluffy and soft, and he whispers, "You know Daddy loves you. C'mon, baby, tell Daddy what you want."

Again Arthur turned back to Claudia. Creeping under the table with her, he gently said, "I'm begging you, baby. Daddy loves you, darlin'."

Claudia stopped shaking her head and looked at him with innocent, horrified eyes as he reached toward her.

He touched her softly on the arm, and Claudia, her teeth starting to chatter, tears coming from her eyes, began to raise her hands slowly, as though she intended to hug the man who had raped her for eleven years of her life.

"I'll give you anything you want," Arthur said quietly. "Please, baby, please. Daddy's not going to hurt you. I love you."

Claudia's hands dropped down and she arched back from her stepfather. Her body began to tremble violently as both Rose and Arthur peered at her. For a moment, her eyes turned from one to the other, and then she shut her eyes on both of them and let out a bone-chilling scream that seemed to come from deep within her body.

Levinsky looked at her with horror. Her face

was ashen, her mouth was wide open with the most painful scream he had ever heard. My God, he thought. I wanted to give her back her mouth, but not like this. I didn't intend this.

Sweat poured down Levinsky's face. He had made a choice to treat Claudia as a client, not as a human being. But now there was a shattered human being before him, and he had to decide if his efforts to prove her sanity had only succeeded in driving her toward a madness from which she might never recover.

SEVEN

That night when Levinsky got home, he found a note from his wife on the kitchen table: *Gone to mall with kids. TV Dinner in freezer. Landlord wants rent check.* he stared at his wife's handwriting. She had a no-nonsense script—exact, legible, letter perfect. Levinsky's own handwriting was a mess, as "the missus" was forever pointing out to him. "How can you expect to ever make something of your life when you can't even write legibly?" she'd ask. And then she'd point her finger at him and say, "You're a mess, Aaron. A hopeless mess. And everything you *touch* becomes a mess."

Levinsky crumpled her note and hurled it at the trash can. He missed the can by a good foot. Of course. Why not? He was a screw-up: with his career, with his marriage, and now with Claudia's case. His wife was right. Everything he touched became a mess.

He took the frozen dinner from the freezer and removed its tinfoil. As a kind of punishment to himself for being such a worthless human being, he contemplated eating the dinner raw. Could he do it? Nah. He'd just break his teeth and then what would he do with the dentist's bills?

For a time, he stood with the dinner in his hands, bereft and mortified. He'd wanted so badly to uncover what Claudia had been concealing. Like a hunt dog, he'd become single-minded with the scent of her secret. Why had he felt compelled to keep pushing, when she had tried so hard and often to let him know that she couldn't handle the pushing? Well, he did know why. He'd wanted to play the hero for her. All his stupid life, he'd believed in the saying "the truth shall set us free." He'd pursued the truth for Claudia as though it were the holy grail. He'd thought if he could give her the truth, make the whole world see it, he could give her back her freedom. But all he'd given her, in the end, was her captivity. To get her to stop screaming in the courtroom, Dr. Morrison had had to inject her with a heavy dose of sedatives. Then Morrison, assisted by Harry the Bailiff, had carried Claudia out to Morrison's car, where she was whisked back to her psychiatric ward.

He tried to picture her now. Was she still asleep, with drugs rushing through her veins? Or was she awake in a room with barred windows, screaming again? He hated to picture her standing at some barred window, the nightmare life of her childhood fresh in her mind. Oh, he'd wanted so much to help her find the tranquility, the grace he'd seen in the nude photograph taken of her at a window without bars.

Suddenly, Levinsky looked down at his frozen dinner. His fingers were going numb with holding it. He stared at the rock-hard turkey slab in its rock-hard gravy. If he stood still all night, the turkey would eventually thaw enough for him to eat it without having to heat it. But meanwhile, he had a client whom he had let down badly sitting in a room with barred windows, alone. And the masochistic act of eating an uncooked TV dinner wasn't going to right any of the wrongs he had done to that client.

Levinsky hurled his frozen dinner toward the trash can. It not only missed by more than the wad of paper had, it actually boomeranged against the kitchen wall and came back toward him, its little frozen peas serving as tiny bullets. But rather than get upset about the mess he'd made and sulk through the night, he decided to take action. He cleaned up the dinner quickly, placed it neatly in the garbage, put his wife's note in the garbage on top of it, and then looked around the room. Not a sign of a mess anywhere, he thought. And an odd feeling came over him. Was it possible for a human being who made messes in his life, to get those messes cleaned up?

Excited by the possibility that perhaps even a forty-year-old could learn to clean up after himself, Levinsky hurried from the kitchen for his coat and briefcase. He could go to Claudia, force the attendant at the hospital to let him in her room. And if it was too late to be her heroic lawyer and give her freedom, he could at least be her not-so-heroic friend and give her comfort.

Levinsky rushed out of his apartment, tore past the landlord who was coming toward him in search of a rent check, and raced out into the night to see if he could clean up the mess he had made of Claudia Draper's mind.

Levinsky followed a woman attendant along the eerie, half-lit corridors of New York County Prison Hospital's psychiatric ward. The patients had all gone to bed, but as he passed their rooms, he could hear them moaning or crying out in their sleep. One woman was singing a strange, high song that made Levinsky shiver.

At last they reached Claudia's door. The attendant unlocked it, let Levinsky enter the tiny, dark room alone, then locked the door behind him. Levinsky turned automatically at the sound of the door being bolted shut and saw the attendant staring at him through a small window on the door. Then he turned back to the room, and as his eyes adjusted to the dim light, he slowly made out the silhouette of Claudia sleeping on a narrow bed.

He didn't want to wake her, so he walked to the edge of her bed and sat down as gently as possible on the mattress. But even the slight movement of the mattress drew Claudia from her sleep. She bolted up in the bed, startled.

Levinsky laid his hand on her arm. "It's me, Aaron," he said softly.

Claudia stared at him, frightened and wide-eyed for a moment, then she seemed to relax as she slowly said, "Aaron," and lay back down.

There was a slur in her voice. Levinsky knew the drugs still hadn't worn off. Maybe that was good. Maybe the drugs could keep her far away from thoughts of her past . . . at least for tonight.

For a few moments, Levinsky sat quietly, not sure whether to let her go back to sleep or try to talk to her. But when he turned toward her face, she was looking more alert. "I'm sorry. I got so wrapped up in being a goddamn lawyer, I forgot all about you."

Claudia pushed her pillow up against her headboard and leaned against it. "Did we lose?" she asked.

Levinsky grimaced. "Not yet . . ."

Claudia shook her head sadly. "Give up, Levinsky," she said quietly. "Maybe they're right. Maybe I am crazy."

"Shh . . . Shhh."

But Claudia had more to say. She lifted herself up from her pillow, took Levinsky's arm, and said, "I didn't tell him to stop."

Levinsky looked at her incredulously. She was blaming *herself* for what that animal had done to her? "You were a little girl," Levinsky told her.

Claudia let go of Levinsky's arm and shifted her gaze toward her barred window. She stared out at the moon for a time, then said, "I just wanted him to love me."

Levinsky nodded. "Everybody wants that."

Still, Claudia didn't seem reassured. She continued to look at the moon, and as she did her eyes grew more frightened. Was she thinking about the things her stepfather had done to her? Levinsky wished he knew what to say to someone about things like rape. He felt at a loss for the right words—if there were any right words. But when Claudia spoke again, it wasn't about the rape, it was about the hearing. "I can't go back tomorrow. I'm afraid . . . I'll go crazy in there again."

"Don't be afraid," Levinsky assured her. And then he went on, looking at her with all the faith and belief and courage he could find in himself and he said, "You're *sane.* You hear me?"

Claudia opened her mouth, as though she was about to contradict him, but then she seemed to see the confidence he was trying to give her with his eyes, and she smiled instead—the kind of lovely, dreamy smile he had only seen in the photograph, never on her face before—and then she turned the smile into a grin and teasingly said, "Hey. You got to go home on the subway."

"Huh?"

Claudia grinned again. "You're supposed to be home with the missus."

Levinsky thought of joking back at her. All his life he had joked back when people joked with him. But tonight, for some reason, he didn't feel like it. He looked at her with utter seriousness and said, "No. I'm supposed to be here."

Claudia nodded after a time, yawned, and then wound herself about his arm and drifted off to sleep. Her hair spilled over Levinsky's lap. He looked at her curls, thought of how she had once chopped them all off in an attempt to change her life. It wasn't very easy to change a life, to put your messes behind you and begin anew. But maybe Claudia and Levinsky could both save themselves. He would take care of her in the courtroom tomorrow. He would be a human being first, and a lawyer second. He wouldn't let her be insane. And maybe she wouldn't let him lose.

For an hour Levinsky sat with Claudia sleeping beside him. He listened to her breaths, steady and calm, as though she trusted him. And with each of her breaths, he became more determined that together they could make everything okay for each other the next day.

At last he rose and walked softly toward the door. The female attendant was still standing with her face pressed to the windowpane, watching him. Big brother—in this case Big Sister—was everywhere in this strange hospital ward. All the intimacy Levinsky had felt with Claudia had actually been a pseudo: intimacy, violated by this woman's suspicious eyes.

Levinsky gave the woman a disgusted glance and went in search of a cafeteria for a cup of coffee. He knew better than to trust a coffee machine.

After getting lost three or four times, Levinsky finally made it to the basement of the hospital where he could smell french fries and day-old barbeque beef. He let his nose, rather than the colored lines on the floor, guide him to a stark cafeteria, where—lo and behold—Dr. Morrison sat at a table shoveling large forkfuls of fruit salad and cottage cheese into his mouth.

The second Levinsky set eyes on Morrison he began thinking about the drugs Morrison had pumped into Claudia's body. It would be just like Morrison to keep those drugs coming, to fill her up with drugs tomorrow morning so that she would seem to the judge like something straight out of *Night of the Living Dead.* And Levinsky was not going to let that happen.

He walked up to the psychiatrist he had come to view as pretentious, self-absorbed, and absolutely full of crap. "Get up."

Morrison could hear the threat in Levinsky's voice, but went on pushing fruit salad into his mouth. "What?" he asked.

"Get up," Levinsky said again. "We have to talk."

Eyeing Levinsky as though he was a pesky fly, Morrison said, "I'm eating."

Not anymore you're not, Levinsky thought, and gave Morrison's tray a shove that sent it—fruit salad and all—flying across the cafeteria.

"See?" Levinsky said. "You're finished."

Morrison glared at Levinsky with hatred but kept his voice calmly professional. "Is there a problem, Mr. Levinsky?" he asked.

"You've drugged my patient within an inch of consciousness."

With an accusatory stare, Morrison said, "After what you put her through today, can you imagine my *not* giving her some sedation?"

Levinsky grimaced. "If she's a zombie tomorrow, I'm going to sue your ass to China and back."

Morrison shook his head slightly to register his disapproval of Levinsky's coarse language, but then said pleasantly, "She'll be fine tomorrow."

Levinsky pointed a finger at the psychiatrist's face. "I want her *lucid.* Not *drugged.*"

Suddenly seeming to forget his role as the well-bred psychiatrist, Morrison pushed Levinsky's finger away from his face and growled, "Don't threaten me, you lawyer son of a bitch!"

Levinsky laughed at Morrison's new mobster tone of voice and turned to leave. As he passed the tray of fruit salad on the floor, he spun around, gave it a kick in Morrison's direction, and called out politely, *"Bon appétit!"*

And with that, he left the cafeteria. He no longer needed a cup of coffee to give him a boost. He was feeling strong again, confident again. He could face whatever he had to face: as a lawyer, and also as a human being.

He left the hospital and jogged over to the subway station that would take him back to Queens and his wife. And he would tell her when he got home that she should stop asking him when he was going to become a success. Because he knew that as long as he was prepared to keep facing the messes life hurled his way, he was already a success.

EIGHT

The sun was shining through the courtroom windows Tuesday morning, casting its light on each of the people in the room. Almost everyone seemed washed out by the light, diminished somehow. The judge squinted as he entered in his somber black robes and quickly signaled Harry the Bailiff to adjust the blinds. Harry did so, but the light still poked its way through the grimy windows, illuminating every participant in the Claudia Draper case.

Frank MacMillan looked worn out, a little bit less the ambitious district attorney, a little bit more the overworked lawyer. Even Dr. Morrison seemed weary and pale this morning. As for Rose Kirk—sitting conspicuously alone in the back of the court—she appeared ten years older than she had the day before. Her face was puffy and haggard, as though she hadn't slept all night, and her head was dropped low with shame.

Claudia, too, looked done in. For one thing, she

was back to wearing her hospital pajamas and robe, but even worse, her eyes were still full of sleep and her head turned slowly, almost dazedly, when Levinsky asked her how she was feeling. She said she was fine, but Levinsky—the one person in the courtroom who appeared energized by the morning light—wondered. Had Morrison given her more drugs?

Judge Murdoch cleared his throat and leaned over the bench. "Mr. Levinsky," he said, "are you ready to proceed?"

Levinsky leaped to his feet. "Yes, your honor. I call the defendant, Claudia Faith Draper."

The judge glanced at Claudia. He could see her exhaustion. "Mrs. Draper," he said kindly, "you can testify from your seat, if you like."

"Why?" Claudia asked.

"I think you might be more comfortable."

But Claudia shook her head with determination. "I'd like to take the stand, please."

"As you like," the judge said curtly.

Claudia moved slowly toward the witness chair. Harry the Bailiff followed after her with a Bible. When she finally reached the chair, she placed her left hand on the Bible and weakly raised her right.

"Do you solemnly swear that the testimony that you shall give in this special proceeding shall be the truth, the whole truth, and nothing but the truth?"

"I do."

Harry nodded. "Be seated, please."

Claudia sank into the chair as Levinsky hurried over to her.

"Mrs. Draper," he began, "do you understand the charge made against you?"

Claudia frowned. "Which charge? The manslaughter charge?"

"Yes. Can you define it for me?"

Again Claudia frowned. Levinsky looked at her, hoping she could remember the sections he had given her to read in the criminal law text he had handed to her at their first meeting. She had told him she'd read them and he believed her. But after all the drugs she'd been given by Morrison yesterday, and after all the stress she'd been through, could her mind plug into her memory of the text?

Claudia's brow unfurrowed. "First-degree manslaughter," she began tentatively. "It's a class-B felony under section 125 point . . . something of the Penal Law." And then she broke off and shook her head. "I'm sorry—I'm—I forgot."

Levinsky glanced sharply at Dr. Morrison, then turned back to Claudia. "Mrs. Draper, were you given any medication in the last twenty-four hours? Sedatives, tranquilizers?"

MacMillan came to his feet. "Objection, your honor," he called out. "If Mr. Levinsky wants medical testimony, he can question Dr. Morrison."

Grimacing, Levinsky looked at the judge. "Your honor," he said, "my client is fighting against the effects of unwanted drugs, drugs intended to dull one's senses. I request an adjournment."

But Claudia shook her head. "No!" she insisted. "I'm all right."

Levinsky looked at her curiously. "Are you *sure*?" he asked quietly.

The judge also gave Claudia a glance. "Mrs. Draper?"

Claudia kept her eyes focused on Levinsky. Softly, but with absolute certainty, she said, "I want to do it now, Aaron."

Levinsky looked at her a moment more, then turned toward the judge and nodded. If Claudia was certain she could do it, he would be just as certain.

"Proceed, Mr. Levinsky," the judge said.

Levinsky began to pace, unaware that he himself was doing a fairly good Perry Mason walk. "Have you conferred with counsel concerning the charge against you?" he asked.

"Yes, several times," Claudia said.

"During these conferences, did you give me all the facts and details constituting your defense to the indictment?"

Claudia nodded. She had told Levinsky everything she could about the killing of "Allen Green." "Yes, I did," she said.

Levinsky stopped pacing. "Can you explain the legal concept of justifiable force?"

Claudia frowned for a moment, then quickly said, "If someone is beating your brains through the back of your head, you're allowed to stop them any way you can."

Levinsky glanced at Judge Murdoch to see what

the judge thought of Claudia's unorthodox—if apt—explanation. The judge had a glimmer of a smile on his lips: he bought it. So Levinsky went on. "Can you tell us the provisions of Article 730?"

"If I lose today," Claudia said confidently, "I'm gone for a year. Sixty days before the year is up, the hospital can ask to keep me. If I lose again, I'm gone for another year. From then on, they can apply to hold me every two years until two-thirds of the maximum sentence. It works out to be sixteen, seventeen years." And then he grinned, raised a finger, and said, "But there's more . . ."

MacMillan came to his feet, evidently not feeling like hearing page after page from a criminal law text. "Your honor—"

But Judge Murdoch immediately cut MacMillan off. "You'll have your cross, Mr. MacMillan." And then he leaned toward Claudia. "What does that mean to you, Mrs. Draper?"

"If they do it right," Claudia said, "those clowns can lock me up in a hospital for the criminally insane forever."

MacMillan stood up again. "Your honor, the witness is exaggerating—"

Claudia gestured toward her legal text over at the defendant's table. "On the table over there is a book called *Criminal Law of New York.* Pages 287 through 298." And then she proudly added, "Look it up."

Levinsky grinned happily at his client, but MacMillan merely rolled his eyes and turned toward the judge. "Your honor, the witness is extending the practical limits of the statute."

But Judge Murdoch just held up his hand to silence MacMillan and turned his attention back to Claudia, who looked up innocently toward the judge and blithely said, "I didn't write the book. The Honorable Eugene R. Canudo, Judge, New York City Criminal Court—"

Again MacMillan voiced an objection. "Your honor—"

The judge held up his hand again. "However it might be executed, Mr. MacMillan, that *is* the statute. As *you* should know."

MacMillan sat down in a huff as the judge turned his attention back to the witness stand. "Proceed, Mr. Levinsky."

Resisting an impulse to stick out his tongue at MacMillan and say "Nyah, nyah, nyah," Levinsky continued with his questioning. "Can you tell me the names of the doctors who examined you?" he asked Claudia.

"Julio Arantes and Herbert Morrison."

"How long was Dr. Arantes's examination?"

"Fifteen minutes," Claudia said, "maybe twenty. He doesn't speak much English."

"Objection," MacMillan called out.

But Judge Murdoch raised his hand, overruling the objection, before MacMillan was even able to make it fully to his feet.

Claudia looked at MacMillan. "Well, he doesn't," she said. And then she added, "His Spanish isn't so hot, either."

MacMillan slid into his seat and stared at the courtroom window with silent anger as Levinsky went on with his questioning. "How long did Dr. Morrison examine you?"

"Fifty, fifty-five minutes," Claudia said. She gave Morrison a sarcastic glance. "He knows more English."

Levinsky walked closely toward her. "Do you accept the findings of the psychiatric examinations given to you at New York County Prison Hospital?"

"I do *not*," Claudia said.

"And do you believe that you're physically and mentally prepared to go on trial?"

"Yes," Claudia said firmly, "I do."

Levinsky smiled at her and she grinned back at him.

"I have no more questions, your honor," Levinsky finally said. And he strolled back to his seat with pleasure. Claudia had done her homework well. He couldn't get over how she had been able to quote the statute. Even when he had been a law student, he hadn't been able to memorize things so easily and state them so impressively.

But as Levinsky sat down at the defendant's table, his pleasure in Claudia's responses turned to anxiety about MacMillan's questioning. Levinsky had shown persuasively that Claudia could behave intelligently and sanely under the right circumstances. MacMillan would be trying to show that under stress, Claudia couldn't control herself. He would want to establish the idea that although

Claudia might understand the charges against her, she couldn't deal with the kind of mental stress a defendant had to bear at a trial. And Levinsky could only hope and trust that Claudia would prove him wrong.

The judge turned toward the district attorney. "Mr. MacMillan?"

MacMillan walked quickly up to the witness stand, then leaned over Claudia solicitously. "Claudia, if you're feeling tired, I'm sure the court would—"

Claudia interrupted MacMillan. "I'm *not* tired," she assured him. "And I would like you to call me Mrs. Draper."

"Very well," MacMillan said.

"When I get tired," Claudia added, "I'll let you know."

MacMillan nodded. "Mrs. Draper—" he began again.

But Claudia interrupted him once more. Leaning toward him as solicitously as he was leaning toward her, she sweetly asked, "Are *you* tired?"

MacMillan smiled at her indulgently, but did straighten up his posture. "Mrs. Draper, how long were you married?"

"Six weeks short of ten years," Claudia said.

"Was this a happy marriage?"

With a shrug, Claudia said, "It had its moments."

"Do you have children from this marriage?" MacMillan asked.

"No, no children."

"Was that by choice, Mrs. Draper?"

Claudia nodded. "Yes."

"Whose choice?"

Annoyed, but still polite, Claudia said, "We agreed."

But MacMillan wasn't letting go of the subject. "You *jointly* agreed?"

Claudia leaned back in her chair and stared at MacMillan. Then—still polite—she said, "I said if I got pregnant, I'd leave him. So he agreed with me."

"So you didn't get pregnant?" MacMillan asked pointedly.

"Yes, I did," Claudia admitted. "We came home from a party and we were a little drunk and I kept putting too much jelly on my diaphragm."

Judge Murdoch turned a little pink at the ears, but MacMillan kept up his personal line of questioning. "And did you leave your husband when you got pregnant?"

"No, I had an abortion."

"Why?" MacMillan asked.

Claudia thought for a second and said, "I don't believe in childhood."

MacMillan decided to change his tack. "Did you love your husband?" he asked.

"I don't know," Claudia said honestly.

MacMillan eyed her keenly and opened his mouth as though to ask her to answer yes or no, but then he closed his mouth again, perhaps realizing that she had given him the only answer she could under oath.

MacMillan took a step back, looked around the

courtroom, then moved on to a new subject. "Where did you move after your marriage collapsed?"

"I moved to 501 East Sixty-sixth Street."

"Is that where you were living when you were arrested?"

Claudia nodded. "Yes."

At the defendant's table, Levinsky began to tense up. MacMillan was trying to steer the conversation toward the subject of Claudia's prostitution. Would Claudia be able to evade the topic? MacMillan was shrewd about backing the witnesses into corners, leading them to talk about subjects they didn't want to talk about. And while MacMillan knew better than to try to directly question Claudia about a crime she hadn't been charged with, he could certainly try to get her to bring up her life as a call girl.

"What was your rent at that address?"

"Twenty-two hundred dollars a month," Claudia said.

MacMillan raised his eyebrows, making sure everyone in the court could see his feigned astonishment at a divorcee's ability to pay such a vast sum in rent, then said, "when you moved to your Sixty-sixth Street apartment, Mrs. Draper, what income did you have?"

"Peter gave me ten thousand dollars when I signed the separation agreement."

"And did you ask your parents for any money?"

Anger flashed in Claudia's eyes. "No," she said.

Immediately, Levinsky jumped to his feet, turned to Judge Murdoch, and said, "Your honor, could

Mr. MacMillan tell us why he's so fascinated with the defendant's finances. Is he planning to sell her a car?"

The judge ignored the laughter that moved through the courtroom and inclined his head toward MacMillan. "Where are you heading, Mr. MacMillan?"

MacMillan smiled icily. "My next group of questions will show you, your honor—if you would indulge me."

The judge, to Levinsky's vast disappointment, nodded. All Levinsky could do was sit down again and pray that MacMillan didn't lead Claudia into a violent explosion.

MacMillan continued. "So, you lived on the ten thousand you got from your husband."

Claudia shook her head. "No, I spent that on furniture and kitchen stuff."

"Well, Mrs. Draper," MacMillan said innocently, "what did you live on?"

Claudia looked toward Levinsky. All Levinsky could do was nod for her to answer the question in the best way she could.

For some time, Claudia sat quietly, and then she looked up brightly at MacMillan and cheerfully said, "Gifts."

Levinsky smiled. Good girl, he thought.

MacMillan shot Claudia a suspicious glance. *"Gifts?"*

"Uh-huh," Claudia said.

"Gifts from *whom*?"

"Friends."

"*Men* friends?" MacMillan asked pointedly.

"Uh-huh."

Levinsky could tell that MacMillan was getting irritated by Claudia's deft fielding of his questions. It was incredible watching the usually cool and calm district attorney start to lose some of his control. Even more wonderful, though, was seeing how absolutely *in* control Claudia was remaining. There wasn't a sign of anger in her responses. In fact, she seemed delighted by her ability to be both cunning and honest at once. She could make one helluva lawyer, Levinsky thought, if she ever makes it out of the loony bin.

"What did these men friends give you?" MacMillan asked Claudia. "Jewelry?"

"Sometimes."

"Furs?"

Claudia smiled proudly. "I got a fox boa once."

MacMillan was not amused. He pressed on. "Did they give you food?"

"Food," Claudia mused. "One guy used to bring caviar; is that what you mean?"

Ignoring Claudia's question, MacMillan said, "Tell me, Mrs. Draper, did you exchange these jewels and furs at the supermarket? Did you offer them to your landlord?"

Claudia shook her head. "No."

"Well," MacMillan said, walking closer to the witness stand, "how did you pay for your food. I assume you didn't live on caviar. Did you use the gifts to pay for your rent?"

Suddenly, Claudia spun around toward Judge

Murdoch and signaled him to move closer to her. Puzzled but obedient, the judge leaned across the bench while Claudia whispered, "Is it legal to take cash gifts?"

The judge wrinkled his brow. "I beg your pardon?"

Claudia went on, relaxing. "If I say to you, 'Stanley, here's five hundred dollars just because I like you,' is that legal?"

The judge thought for a moment, then said, "Yes, that's legal."

Claudia grinned her appreciation to the judge, then spun back to MacMillan and said, "A lot of the gifts were cash."

"I see," MacMillan said. "And these cash gifts from these men friends were enough to pay your expenses?"

"Uh-huh."

MacMillan nodded to himself, then gave Claudia a cunning glance and quietly asked, "And what did these men expect in return for these gifts?"

Instantly, Levinsky came to his feet. If MacMillan thought he could label Claudia a prostitute when she had not been indicted for prostitution, he had another think coming. He called out to the judge, "Is counsel for the people leading to—"

MacMillan cut Levinsky off. "Your honor," he said, "I have not used the word *fee.*"

The judge ruled in MacMillan's favor. "I'll permit an answer," he said.

MacMillan shot Levinsky a triumphant look. If he could bring Claudia to freely label *herself* a prostitute, then the subject of her prostitution could be explored eagerly and avidly by MacMillan. all he had to do was be careful not to declare her a prostitute himself until she admitted to being one.

Levinsky dropped into his seat, nervous and worried whether Claudia would be able to keep her composure during the badgering MacMillan had in store for her. Would she be able to resist perjuring herself? He knew MacMillan was determined to lead her into a discussion of her life as a call girl, and that he had the legal savvy to do this without seeming to lead the witness. Would Claudia find a way to evade him?

MacMillan smiled at Claudia. "What did these men expect in return for these cash gifts?" he asked innocently.

"Friendship," Claudia said.

"What *kind* of friendship?"

Levinsky jumped to his feet again. "Objection! The question is vague and misleading."

"Sustained," the judge said.

Levinsky sat down, but remained ready to spring into action. If MacMillan was determined to walk this tightrope, then Levinsky had to keep pushing him off of it.

MacMillan rephrased his question. "These men who gave you gifts, did they expect you to talk to them?"

"Sure," Claudia said.

"You listened to them?"

Claudia rolled her eyes. "God, yes."

MacMillan pushed further. "You did them favors?" he suggested.

Like a jack-in-the-box, Levinsky was instantly back on his feet. "Your honor—"

But the judge overruled his objection with a wave of his hand.

MacMillan repeated his question. "You did them favors?"

Levinsky sat down again as Claudia nodded and said, "Uh-huh."

"What kind of favors?" MacMillan asked pleasantly.

Up bounced Levinsky. "Objection! On same grounds."

MacMillan kept talking as the Judge ignored Levinsky. "What kind of favors did you do in return for these gifts?"

Furiously, Levinsky pounded on the table. "The defendant has not been charged with—"

Now, the judge glared at Levinsky as, once more, he waved his hand to silence him.

MacMillan leaned closely over Claudia. "*What kind of favors?*" he shouted.

For a second, Claudia pulled back from the force of MacMillan's questioning, but then she collected herself and glanced around the courtroom. The judge was still staring angrily at Levinsky, who was still standing up in protest of MacMillan's question to Claudia. Claudia eyed the judge a moment, then eyed her lawyer. Finally, she turned her attention to the district attorney, who was glowering at her.

Coolly, Claudia leaned back in her chair and said, "Let's stop all the bullshit and get to the point. You want to know what I do for a living? Ask me!"

Oh no, Levinsky thought, sinking into his seat. Oh please, Claudia, no!

Claudia stared at MacMillan straight in the eye. "I get four hundred for a straight lay," she said matter-of-factly, "two hundred for a hand job, and five hundred for head. If you wanna wear my panties, that's another hundred. No whips, no ropes, no spikes. I've got liquor and grass. Anything else, you bring your own."

Levinsky's chin sank into the palms of his hands as he watched Judge Murdoch's eyes widen and his ears turn a deep red. Why is she doing this? Levinsky wondered. Judge Murdoch's probably going to have a cardiac arrest, die on the spot, and we're gonna have to start all over again.

But Claudia calmly continued outlining the details of her job as though she were an engineer explaining how to construct a bridge. "It works like this: you call me, we make a date, I look you over, and if I like you, we make a deal." And then she let her voice drop low as she spoke to each man in the courtroom. "And darlin', I am *worth* the trouble, take my word for it. If you want the best. *Do* you want the best?"

Levinsky's chin came up from his palms, as if he were hearing a siren song. Even Dr. Morrison leaned closer in his seat to listen.

Claudia went on, her voice husky and sensuous,

her eyes hypnotically taking in MacMillan, Morrison, Levinsky, even Judge Murdoch. "I am talking about taking your body to heaven and sending your mind south," she assured the men. "I am talking about spoiling you so bad you'll hate every other woman you touch. I'm talking about baby pink nipples that get hard when you breathe on them. I'm talking about my skin on your skin and my tongue in your ear. I'm talking about indulging your every fantasy, and showing you what dreams are made of, and then giving you those dreams, one by one, just for all, all for you, nobody but you."

MacMillan stared unblinkingly at Claudia as she eyed him keenly. "Do you get all that, darlin'?" she asked. "Would you like that, baby? Do you *get* what I'm tellin' you?" And then her eyes flashed around the courtroom. "Do you *all* get what I'm tellin' you?"

Every man present certainly did. There was a long pause, followed by a great deal of embarrassed coughing, crossing of legs, and hands being thrust into pockets.

Claudia leaned over toward the extremely embarrassed face of Judge Murdoch and sweetly asked, "Can he bust me for that?"

The judge, who appeared to be in a state of shock, tried to answer Claudia's question. "Can he—er, no, he can't . . . bust you."

As for MacMillan, his face was flushed, but he appeared determined to pull himself together with sarcasm. "Very enlightening, Mrs. Draper," he said to Claudia.

Claudia grinned, fully aware that she had gotten to MacMillan a lot more than he would ever admit—even to himself. "I thought you'd like it," she said lightly.

MacMillan cleared his throat and attempted to move on. "And how long did you perform these favors?"

Claudia thought for a moment, then said, "thirty-five months, twenty-four days."

"Can you tell us *why* you performed these favors for men?"

Claudia gave MacMillan a look that clearly read, "Oh, come off it," and then said, "For a hundred thousand dollars a year . . . net."

MacMillan glanced toward Rose Kirk, who was watching the proceedings with anxious eyes. "Did you ever ask your parents for money?" he asked.

"No," Claudia said flatly.

"Do you believe they would have refused to lend or give you the money?"

Claudia looked quickly at her mother, then back to MacMillan. "They would have given it to me," she said after some time.

MacMillan feigned surprise. "But nonetheless you preferred a life of exchanging favors for gifts."

"It hurts less to sell yourself to strangers," Claudia said quietly.

In the back of the courtroom, Rose began to weep. MacMillan looked her way for a moment, then turned back to Claudia and asked, "If you were in the same position today, would you make the same choice?"

Levinsky came to his feet. "Your honor," he said, "she's *not* in the same position."

But the judge only gave Levinsky a sharp glance and said, "I'd like an answer."

Claudia thought a few seconds, then said, "I might."

"You would return to a life like that rather than ask your parents for money?" MacMillan inquired.

Shrugging, Claudia said, "I don't know. Probably. Either way, you pay." And then she looked at her weeping mother and softly added, "If you ever want to listen, Mama, I can try to explain it."

MacMillan tried to continue over Rose Kirk's crying. "Mrs. Draper, would you describe your courtroom behavior these past days as normal?"

"Would you describe the circumstances as normal?" Claudia quickly shot back.

MacMillan gave Claudia a smug look. "My job is to ask the questions. It is *your* obligation to answer them."

"Okay," Claudia said. "Ask."

"Well," MacMillan began, "yesterday the hearing was adjourned because you were . . . no longer able to participate."

Claudia's eyes flashed, but she held her composure. "Look," she said, "the truth is, I didn't have a nifty childhood. Poor me. So what? Life sucks!" And then she looked around the courtroom, her eyes taking in each person, and continued. "You all had a good time yesterday watching me—and my stepfather—squirm. Okay. It's out, it's over, it's a fact of life, I'll *handle* it. But the point is: it's not relevant to what is going on in here."

Levinsky had to tuck his hands under himself to keep from cheering. Way to go, he thought, bring those Dodgers all the way back home to Ebbett's Field, kiddo!

But MacMillan was already moving on to a new tack. As though he were a psychiatrist himself, he leaned close to Claudia and soothingly said, "Mrs. Draper, *you* don't trust me, do you?"

With an incredulous look on her face, Claudia said, "What are you, crazy?" And then catching her unintentional irony, she laughed and said, "Sorry. That's *your* question, isn't it?"

MacMillan didn't answer. Instead, he gave Claudia a condescending stare and went on with his questions. "Have I ever done anything to harm you, Mrs. Draper?"

Claudia snorted. "I don't *believe* this. You're trying to *put me away*."

"You don't believe that I have no personal motive and that I'm simply doing my job?" MacMillan asked.

"Your job is to get me," Claudia said with conviction. "Your job is to put me in a hospital." And then she raised an eyebrow and added, "I don't know . . . I guess I'm dumb. I take that personally."

"And you believe Dr. Morrison is acting out of a personal motive, don't you?" MacMillan asked, hammering away as best he could at Claudia's alleged paranoia.

But Claudia shook her head. "No," she said, "I'm sure he believes what he believes. He thinks whores are girls who hang out on Eighth Avenue and stick needles in their arms. Whores aren't nice white girls from nice white homes. He knows that; he knows that as sure as his wife is home cleaning the oven."

Morrison shifted in his seat as Claudia turned toward him with a mischievous yet cunning grin. "But what if he's wrong?" she went on, her gaze fixed on Morrison. "What if his wife is balling the insurance salesman? What if he doesn't know his ass from his elbow? What if he's just an asshole with the power to lock me up?" And then she leaned over the witness stand and called out to Morrison, "What if that's all he is—an asshole with power?"

With a florid face and furious eyes, Dr. Morrison stood up and turned to Judge Murdoch. "Your honor, forgive me for interrupting, but in her paranoid way, she sees my testimony as an attack on her, and she's lashing out in retaliation."

Claudia sat back in her chair. "Hah!"

Morrison kept his eyes fixed on Judge Murdoch. "I believe the pressure of this proceeding is doing serious harm to the patient, and she should be taken back to the hospital."

"Ah," Claudia said with amusement, "he wants to take me home."

Dr. Morrison took a deep breath, as though he were working very hard to keep his temper in check, and went on: "Your honor, I believe she's very close to the hysteria she demonstrated in the courtroom yesterday. She's my patient and I'm responsible for her."

Claudia touched her heart as though she were extremely moved. "He wants to take care of me," she said.

At last Morrison spun toward Claudia, his eyes crackling with fury. Walking toward her, he said icily, "I know precisely what she's going through and precisely how to treat it."

Levinsky leaped to his feet. "Your honor," he called out as Morrison continued advancing toward Claudia, "is Dr. Morrison threatening the witness?"

"Doctor," Judge Murdoch said solemnly, "take your seat, please."

But Morrison kept walking up to the witness stand. "For her sake, I insist that this patient—"

But Morrison kept walking up to the witness stand. "For her sake, I insist that this patient—"

"I said, take your seat!" the judge commanded.

Morrison looked at the judge with angry, wild eyes, then seemed to catch himself, correct himself. At last, he meekly returned to his seat.

"Continue, Mr. MacMillan," the judge said.

MacMillan nodded and turned again to Claudia. "Mrs. Draper, do you trust his honor, the court?"

"More than I trust you," Claudia said evenly.

"Do you trust your own attorney, Mr. Levinsky?"

Eyeing Levinsky carefully, Claudia quietly said, "As lawyers go, he's all right."

Levinsky grinned as MacMillan went on. "And do you trust Mrs. Kirk, your mother?"

"My mother?"

"Do you trust your mother?" MacMillan asked again.

Claudia looked at the weeping, white-haired woman in the back of the courtroom. "No," she said after a few seconds.

MacMillan shook his head as if he were personally saddened by this daughter's inability to trust her mother, and then said, "Is there *anyone* in this courtroom you do trust, without qualification?"

Claudia glanced around for a moment. Her eyes fastened on Harry the Bailiff. She looked at him with interest for a time, then pointed in his direction and said, "I trust him."

MacMillan spun to see where Claudia's finger was pointing and stared at the bailiff with shock. "You're pointing to Officer Harry Haggerty."

Claudia nodded. "Yes."

Harry the Bailiff, although a bit embarrassed by the sudden attention, seemed pleased to be considered worthy of Claudia's trust, but MacMillan seemed angered by it. "The only person in this room you trust is Officer Haggerty?" he cried out indignantly.

"He can't hurt me," Claudia said bluntly. "You can, the judge can, Morrison can, and"—looking keenly at her mother—"she can. I don't trust people who can hurt me; not anymore."

"You believe your mother wants to hurt you?" MacMillan asked.

Claudia sighed, as though she knew MacMillan was constitutionally incapable of understanding what she had to say. But she still tried to explain. "She doesn't *want* to hurt me, but . . ."

Suddenly, in a stricken voice, Rose called out, "I don't want to hurt you, darling. I *never* wanted to hurt you."

Claudia glanced down at the floor of the courtroom. Levinsky watched her sadly. He could understand her dilemma. She wanted to trust her mother—everyone *wants* to trust—but trust was something that once lost had to be found again before it could be given. Claudia could no more believe in her mother than she could believe in Santa Claus. It didn't matter a damn whether Rose Kirk had wanted to hurt her daughter; she *had* hurt her. She had lost the right to be trusted. And no words out of Rose's mouth were going to give her back that trust.

"You don't believe your mother wants to help you?" MacMillan asked Claudia.

Claudia looked up from the floor, eyed MacMillan with anger for a moment, then said, "Of *course* she wants to help me. You *all* want to help me." And then she pointed at Harry again, and said, "Except for Harry. Harry doesn't give a damn."

MacMillan frowned with puzzlement, but he went on. "Mrs. Draper, do you believe your mother loves you?"

Rose cried out, "Of *course* I love you."

Claudia wiped her hand across her forehead. "There's that word again. . . ." Her eyes flashed at

MacMillan. "You stand up there asking do you love your daughter and she says yes and you think you've asked something real, and she thinks she's said something real. You think because you toss the word *love* around like a Frisbee we're all going to get warm and runny? No!" And then she sighed, sank into her chair, and quietly said, "Sometimes people love you so much their love is like a gun that keeps firing straight into your head. They love you so much you go right into a hospital."

The courtroom was silent for a few seconds as Claudia stared at her mother and whispered, "Mama, you say you love me, but you gave me away."

"Baby, I didn't *know,*" Rose said imploringly.

"Mama," Claudia said with certainty, "you didn't *want* to know."

MacMillan glanced from Rose to Claudia, and then asked hesitantly, "Mrs. Draper, I'm a little confused . . . but . . . *do* you love your mother?"

"Oh, Christ," Claudia muttered.

But MacMillan couldn't let go of the idea that life was some kind of Burt Bacharach song in which love makes the world go round. "The question was," MacMillan said, "*do* you love your mother?"

Claudia looked at her heartbroken, pathetic mother, then looked back at MacMillian. "Yes," she said emotionlessly, "I love my mother." And then she shrugged and added, "So what?"

MacMillan had no response to her question, so

he ignored it and turned to the judge. "I have no further questions, your honor."

Judge Murdoch glanced at Claudia. "You may step down."

Claudia, seemingly perplexed by the abrupt end to MacMillan's cross-examination, looked confused as she walked back to the defendant's table where Levinsky was waiting for her.

"You were fine," Levinsky whispered. "You told the truth."

But Claudia still seemed perplexed as she sat down beside her attorney.

MacMillan remained up at the front of the courtroom. "Your honor," he said, "I'd like to recall Dr. Morrison."

As Levinsky watched Morrison strut to the stand, Claudia tugged his jacket sleeve and said, "Levinsky? I don't think anybody *heard* me."

Levinsky wasn't sure how to reply. He knew what she meant; she didn't think anyone in the courtroom was able to understand the idea that she would be insane if she *did* trust those who had hurt her so badly in the name of love. And for all Levinsky knew, she was right to be worried about this. So he squeezed her arm and whispered, "*I* heard you."

At the witness stand, MacMillan was beginning to question Dr. Morrison. "In view of the defendant's testimony, doctor, and all that's happened in the court, have you changed your opinion as to her capacity?"

Dr. Morrison folded his arms across his chest and proudly said, "Absolutely not."

Suddenly, Claudia leaped to her feet. "Wait a second!" she yelled. "Wait one goddamn second!"

"Mrs. Draper," the judge said as a warning.

Claudia whirled on the judge, "*Capacity?* Did they examine *him* for his capacity?" And then she gave the judge a suspicious once-over. "Did they examine *you*? I know a judge who jerks off under his robe, they never gave *him* a test."

The judge's eyes opened wide, but he let Claudia continue her rampage. She rushed over to MacMillan, pointing a finger at him. "Did they examine *you* for your capacity?" And then she gestured at her mother. "Did they examine *her*?"

At last the judge held up his hand. "Mrs. Draper, you're not on the stand."

Claudia ran toward the bench. "Then *put* me back on the goddamn stand until I *convince* you," she pleaded. "Don't whip me with your rules. While you're playing with your rules, the meter is running out on my life!"

The judge sighed. "Mrs. Draper . . ."

Levinsky came to his feet. Looking the judge deeply in the eyes, speaking as passionately as he could, he said, "Please, your honor. Give her a chance to speak."

The judge kept his eyes even on Levinsky for a moment, as if he were looking for something in Levinsky's gaze. Then he nodded.

Claudia spun toward Levinsky. She seemed shocked, amazed, and delighted all at once as she stared at her attorney with a smile that Levinsky could have sworn showed the beginnings of trust. . . .

She turned to the judge again and began: "I know I'm supposed to be a good little girl for my mother and father, and an obedient wife to my husband, and stick out my tongue for the doctor, and lower my head for the judge. I know all that; I know what you expect me to do. But I am *not* just a wife or a hooker or a patient or a defendant. Can't you *get* that? You think giving blow jobs for five hundred dollars is nuts. Well, I know women who marry men they despise so they can drive a Mercedes and spend summers in the Hamptons."

Now Claudia spun sharply toward her mother and looked Rose keenly in the eyes. "I know women," she went on, "who peddle their daughters to hang on to their husbands, so don't judge my blow jobs. They're sane."

The judge leaned over the bench. He opened his mouth for a second, appeared about to censure Claudia for her bold language, then seemed to reconsider, and closed his mouth again.

Claudia continued, this time taking in the entire courtroom. "I knew what I was doing every goddamn minute. And I am responsible for it. I lift my skirt, I am responsible; I go down on my knees, I am responsible. If I play the part you want me to play, if I play sick, I won't be responsible. Poor, sick Claudia, she needs our help. I won't play that part. I won't give you that out. I won't be another picture in your heads. 'Claudia the nut.' I won't be nuts for you. Do you get what I'm telling you?"

Now she took a step toward the witness stand and pointed straight at Morrison. "He can sign a piece of paper saying I'm nuts, but it's only a piece of paper. You can't make me nuts that way, no matter how many times you sign it."

She dropped her arm, took a deep breath, then looked at her mother once more. "And no matter how many times you say it," she told Rose, "you can't make me nuts."

Rose shook her head, but Claudia kept going, turned away from her mother and looked again at Judge Murdoch. "Or you," she said firmly. "Get it straight." And then she cried out with both conviction and yearning: *"I won't be nuts for you!"*

For a long time, the courtroom was silent as everyone watched Claudia walk quietly and solemnly back to the defense table where she sat down beside Levinsky.

Judge Murdoch stared intently at her, as if he were struggling towards some kind of evaluation. Finally, he turned to the district attorney and calmly said, "Proceed, Mr. MacMillan."

"Dr. Morrison," MacMillan asked, "do you *still* believe she lacks the capacity to stand trial?"

Morrison's face was granite hard. "Yes, I do."

MacMillan nodded, and then went to the prosecutor's table and sat down as the judge glanced at Levinsky to see if he wished to cross-examine Morrison. "Mr. Levinsky?" the judge asked.

Levinsky started to stand up, but Claudia grabbed his arm, shook her head, and said, "Forget it, it's useless."

For a second, Levinsky thought this over, and then decided she was right. Morrison was one of those people who formed an opinion and kept with it to the grave. So Levinsky said, "I have no questions, your honor," and sat down again.

The judge turned to Morrison. "You may step down, doctor."

As Morrison walked haughtily back to his seat, the judge looked over at MacMillan. "Do you rest?" he asked.

With a nod, MacMillan said, "The People rest, your honor."

Now the judge turned to Levinsky, who rose, sighed, pushed a hand through his unruly hair, and said, "Your honor, the defendant is a pain in the ass. Excuse me."

The judge gave Levinsky an alarmed stare, but Levinsky went on as if he didn't notice it. "She is irritating, obnoxious, loud. She disturbs the peace. But no matter how irritating she may be, we must not equate unpleasantness with mental illness." And then he glanced around the courtroom, shrugged, and added, "The defense rests."

The judge waited until Levinsky had taken his seat, and then he said, "Mr. Levinsky, if the defendant would permit an examination by an independent psychiatrist, I'd consider adjourning this hearing for . . . fourteen days."

Levinsky started to rise again, but MacMillan

beat him to his feet and called out, "Your honor, People would object. Might I point out that, for the record, the defense has rested."

The judge mused on this. "You say People would object, Mr. MacMillan?"

MacMillan nodded. "Yes, your honor."

The judge sat for a few seconds silently. He glanced at Dr. Morrison, glanced at Claudia, even glanced over at Harry the Bailiff. At last, he spoke. "I'm going to call a brief recess," he said. "Just a few moments to gather my thoughts. Stay seated." And then he left the courtroom, his somber black robe trailing behind him as he walked. The court recorder quickly followed.

Levinsky turned to Claudia with a reassuring smile. "It's a good sign," he told her. "He hasn't made up his mind."

But Claudia seemed less hopeful. "Can we get an appeal on this?" she asked nervously.

Before Levinsky could answer, Rose Kirk walked up to her daughter and hesitantly said her name.

Claudia and Levinsky both turned toward Rose, who stood over them with a fearful, apologetic look on her face. Immediately, Claudia stood up and went to her mother, as Rose said, "Your father . . . Arthur . . . couldn't come."

"I'm sorry I yelled at you, Mama," Claudia said.

Rose managed a brave smile. "I hope you win, sweetheart. I hope you get whatever you want, for the rest of your life."

Claudia reached toward her mother. "Let me touch you, Mama," she whispered.

But Rose took a step back and began to cry. "I'm so ashamed," she said at last.

Claudia shook her head and held her mother tightly in her arms. "I still love you, Mama," she said, "to the moon and down again and around the world and back again. . . ."

Suddenly, the judge's door opened. Rose and Claudia moved apart at the sound, but instead of Judge Murdoch appearing, they saw the court reporter, who walked quickly over to her keyboard and and sat down, her fingers poised to type.

"It won't be long now, Mama," Claudia said. "Why don't you go take your seat?"

Meekly, Rose nodded. "I will. Thank you."

Levinsky opened up his briefcase and began arranging his papers as Claudia watched her frail, tired mother walk slowly to the back of the courtroom.

At last, Claudia turned back to the defense table, started to sit down, then stopped and pointed at something that caught her eye in Levinsky's briefcase. She reached her hand into the case and pulled out the nude photograph of herself that Levinsky had removed from her underwear drawer a few days back.

Levinsky's face immediately turned beet red as Claudia looked at him with amusement. "You could tall it larceny," he said at last. "I'd call it bad manners."

Claudia laughed and handed him the picture

back. "Consider it your fee,." And then she asked, "You want me to sign it?"

"What would you say?" Levinsky asked quietly.

"Oh, something that would get you in real big trouble if the missus ever found it."

Levinsky rolled his eyes and wryly echoed her: "The missus."

Suddenly, Claudia's face became serious, even a little red, as she leaned over to her lawyer and said, "You're okay, Levinsky. Even though you think I'm a pain in the ass."

Maybe to another man, the words might not have meant much. But to Levinsky, they meant a helluva lot. They—and the nude photograph—were the greatest gifts he'd ever received as a lawyer . . . or as a person.

The courtroom went quiet. Judge Murdoch was entering. He went quickly up to the bench, sat down, and immediately began to speak. "The court is concerned that the defendant has not supplied any expert medical testimony on her behalf," he began. "This is a critical flaw in the defendant's case. Nor has the defendant's behavior in this courtroom inspired the confidence of the Bench."

Levinsky's heart sank. Was it all going away? Was all the work he and Claudia had put into this hearing for nothing?

The judge continued. "On the other hand, the court is not satisfied that the options expressed by the medical witness Morrison are completely persuasive."

For a few moments the judge paused, as though

he were still wrestling with his decision, while Claudia and Levinsky sat at the edge of their chairs staring at him earnestly. But finally he went on. "I'm torn between my feelings as a man, my conviction that Mrs. Draper may not be strong enough to undergo a trial—and my duty as a judge—my obligation to honor the law and to give our citizens, even our fragile citizens, their day in court."

Again, the judge went silent. This time, he picked up a pencil from his bench, tapped it for a while, then looked up at Claudia and said, "Therefore—I grant the defense their motion to controvert, and I will release the defendant on her own recognizance to await trial on the felony charge of manslaughter in the first degree."

Immediately, MacMillan leaped angrily to his feet. "Your honor," he called out, "the defendant is charged with manslaughter. The People request a high bail."

The judge stared at MacMillan for a time, and then, by way of response, banged his gavel and said, "Court dismissed."

Claudia jumped up from her chair and thrust her arms into the air with triumph. "All right!" she shouted out. And then, with a wink to Judge Murdoch: "Thanks, Stanley!"

Levinsky rose beside her and almost stumbled as she grabbed him hard around the waist and gave him an exuberant bear hug. Oh, if "the missus" could see him now, he thought happily.

Suddenly, Claudia began running toward the

front exit of the courtroom. Levinsky, all smiles, watched her as she spun around at the door and called out, "See you in court, Levinsky!"

With a shrug, Levinsky called back, "I don't know. You did okay by yourself today."

Claudia grinned. "Yeah, I did," she said with pleasure. "Maybe I'll change professions."

Levinsky started walking toward her, his briefcase banging along the chairs in the court as he moved. "So where're you going?" he asked.

"Out!" Claudia shouted gleefully. And then she was off, pushing past people in the corridor of the courthouse, bursting out the door with triumph.

Levinsky stood at the top of the courthouse steps, the New York sun blazing down at him, as he watched Claudia race joyfully, childlike, down the steps and into the street. Her hospital pajamas and oversize robe blew in the autumn wind as she stared with wonder at the city all around her.

The street was full of fast-moving people: Jews, blacks, Presbyterians, Hare Krishnas, businessmen, hustlers, hookers, housewives, and vagrants. Claudia's heart in hiding moved out toward all of them. She watched with amazement as bag people searched the garbage cans for food, as couples pushed their tongues into each other's mouths for love, as street vendors screamed on the corner for money. Everyone was free to do as they pleased, and now she was, too.

Some of the people out on the street stared at Claudia, but most accepted her as one more homeless soul. She walked along proudly, curiously, and when she came across a bag woman, she smiled widely and the lady smiled back. They were sisters in this city, two brave wanderers searching for life.

EPILOG

On January 15, 1986, Claudia Draper was tried in the State Supreme Court, New York County, on a charge of manslaughter in the first degree. She was defended by Aaron Levinsky and was acquitted. She is now attending law school at New York University.

In March of that year, Mr. and Mrs. Kirk marked their thirty-second wedding anniversary. There was no celebration.

On June 5, 1986, Herbert Morrison resigned from the staff of New York County Prison Hospital. He was then appointed deputy commissioner of mental hygiene for the state of New York.